C

20-07-13

GW00854094

2007

Blood and Grass

CORBA SUNMAN

Western

NDON

ISBN 0 7090 7513 8

Robert Hale Limited
Clerkenwell House
Clerkenwell Green
London EC1R 0HT

Typeset by
Derek Doyle & Associates, Liverpool.
Printed and bound in Great Britain by
Antony Rowe Limited, Wiltshire

ONE

It was after sunset when Travis Fenner rode into the cattle town of Brushwood in Kansas and stabled his trail-weary black in the livery barn. He walked along the wide main street to find a hash house, for he had not eaten since leaving the herd just after dawn to scout the last miles of the long trail up from Texas. A Texan himself, like the rest of his Big F crew, he was looking forward to settling in on the vast HF cattle ranch in Kansas that had been left to him and his brother Albie by their uncle, Henry Fenner, whose death marked the passing of the older generation of Fenners. Their father, Joseph, had lived in Texas all his life, building up the Big F ranch, while Uncle Henry had moved north to Clayton County in Kansas to establish his own cattle empire. Now the holdings had passed to the two younger Fenners, and Travis had taken the opportunity to pull stakes in Texas and head for a new life in Kansas.

He found a restaurant that was near to closing and entered with tinkling spurs, a big broad-shouldered man wearing shotgun chaps scratched by brush and covered in trail dust. His green shirt and yellow bandanna added colour to his austere appearance and he was wearing a black leather vest. His boots were scuffed and slightly down-at-heel but his spurs were silver inlaid. A cartridge belt, its loops filled with glinting shells, encircled his lean waist. The cutaway holster on his right thigh contained a bone-handled .45 Colt pistol. His strong features and jutting chin gave him the appearance of a man who could take care of himself in any situation.

Fenner paused in the doorway and glanced around with keen brown eyes that missed nothing. He took off his wide-brimmed black Stetson and slapped it against his thigh to shake off the dust. There was a vacant table in a corner near to the kitchen door and he approached it, to be confronted by a tired-looking waitress who was holding an order pad at the ready. Sitting down at the table, he was giving his order when one of the four men at the next table got up quickly and lurched unsteadily against the waitress, thrusting her to one side. She staggered and almost lost her balance, uttering a cry of shock as she hit the wall and bounced back towards Fenner's table.

The big man causing the disturbance grasped the waitress by a shoulder and thrust her out of his way. He gazed down at Fenner, shoulders hunched, his fist-damaged features alive with deadly resolution. He was a man in his late thirties, powerfully built, dressed in black range garb, even to his neckerchief and Stetson. A black leather gunbelt around his waist was adorned with a black-handled pistol, over which his right hand hovered menacingly.

'Where you from, stranger?' His voice sounded as if he had swallowed a handful of gravel.

'Texas,' Fenner replied, 'if it's any of your business.' He

looked at the waitress, who was standing in the background rubbing her shoulder, resignation on her work-worn features. 'Did he hurt you, Miss?' he demanded.

'I'm all right.' She nodded, her gaze seeming to warn him to pull in his horns.

'I'm talking to you,' the big man rapped. He reached out with his left hand and pushed the girl in the face, thrusting her away so violently she sprawled over a table at her back and fell to the floor.

Fenner gained his feet in a surge of bunching muscles, a move the big man was waiting for because he drew his pistol the instant Fenner moved. Then he stopped with his weapon still pointing at the floor. Fenner's gun muzzle was prodding him in the belly. He heard the three clicks of the weapon being cocked and opened his fingers without being told. The thud of his pistol hitting the floor sounded like the knell of doom in his ears. He gazed into Fenner's narrowed eyes, now sparkling with fury, and the first sharp pang of awareness that he had overplayed his hand stabbed through him.

'You got a way with women I don't cotton to,' Fenner gritted. 'I've a notion to finish the job someone started on you and complete the change your face is begging for. I'm not looking for trouble but I draw a line at your behaviour and, Mister, you sure have overstepped the mark.'

Fenner's right hand moved with the speed of a striking rattlesnake. His gunhand swung upwards and he hit the big man with a back-handed blow that laid the foresight of his .45 across the right temple. The man staggered, his hands reaching out to grasp at Fenner, but the heavy pistol rose and fell again, chopping down like an axe. The man groaned and dropped heavily to the floor. Fenner backed off, his attention switching to the men at the table from which his assailant had arisen.

Three hard faces were regarding him in shocked amazement and a tight grin flitted across Fenner's lips. He could imagine that they were accustomed to their pard accosting strangers, but not to witnessing the downfall of their pet bully.

'If one of you can talk then I'd be obliged if you'll tell me the name of this bruiser,' Fenner said. 'He ain't got much sense, bracing a stranger the way he did, so I reckon he won't be smart enough to take a pistol-whipping without wanting to come back at me again, probably from behind.'

'He'll certainly come back at you,' one of the men said, grinning. 'He's Bud Snark, the town marshal. You made a bad mistake tangling with him, stranger. He's killed men for doing less. Your best bet is to grab your horse and split the breeze out of here. Snark is real mean when it comes to settling a score.'

Fenner glanced down at the inert man. 'He ain't wearing a badge,' he observed.

'You wouldn't have attacked him if you'd seen a badge. Snark likes playing games, and reckons strangers are fair targets. He likes nothing better than fighting. There ain't many around who can handle him, and if you've got the savvy that should go with your ability then right now you oughta be pounding the trail out of Brushwood 'stead of giving Snark time to get back on his feet. He'll tear the town apart to get his hands on you, so split the breeze.'

'I ain't riding through. I'm Travis Fenner, here to take over my uncle's HF spread, and I plan to be around for a long time. No two-bit town bully is gonna run me out.

Snark has got more trouble on his plate than he's ever handled before, and if he has any sense, which I doubt, he'll be the one to start running.'

Fenner holstered his gun with a slick movement and bent to pick up Snark's pistol. He laid it on the table and sat down again, his gaze lifting to the waitress, who was standing hip-shot, her face expressing a blend of fear and astonishment.

'Did I finish giving you my order?' he enquired. 'I'm near to starving. If you're all right then I'd admire to get some service. The smell of food is aggravating my stomach.'

She smiled wanly and hurried into the kitchen. Fenner heaved a sigh as he regarded the prostrate Snark, who was beginning to stir, but his attention was attracted by a big man who suddenly emerged from the kitchen and his eyes narrowed at the sight of a double-barrelled shotgun in the newcomer's hands. Big himself, and accustomed to being around big men, Fenner found himself looking at a small giant. The man, wearing a stained white apron, stood at least fives inches over six feet and bulked large in proportion, his body heavily muscled.

'Where's Snark?' he demanded. 'I've warned that sonofabitch about causing trouble in here.' He spotted the town marshal lying on the floor and his shock was chased away by the grin that appeared on his heavy face. 'Hey, who did that to him?' he demanded. His gaze fixed on Fenner and took in the gun lying on the table. 'Say, you better be riding out before Snark wakes up.' He looked at the table where the three men were sitting. 'Arlen, what's the matter with you? Ain't you warned this stranger about Snark? Do you want another killing in town?'

'I warned him,' one of the trio said – a thin, dark-haired man whose face was intensely expressioned. 'Seems Snark picked on the wrong man this time. This one is a stranger who plans on sticking around for a long time. He's the nephew of Henry Fenner and he's come to take over HF.'

Fenner looked at Arlen, and was surprised to see a deputy sheriff badge pinned to the man's shirt front, partially hidden by his jacket. Arlen grinned at the expression of surprise that flitted across Fenner's face.

'You don't got to worry about my department,' he said. 'I saw what happened. It was clearly a case of self-defence, and Snark wouldn't welcome any interference from me. He'll wanta handle you himself, when he's in a fit state to consider it. Take my advice and don't let him get behind you.'

'He ain't managed to see my back since I whaled the tar outa him for bullying my waitresses.' The big man with the shotgun grinned and lowered his fearsome weapon. 'I'm Al Krone, Fenner. Glad to know you, mister. Any time you want a meal you can come in here and get it for free. Men who can best Snark are thin on the ground, and we got to stick together.'

'I'm Travis Fenner, and like the deputy says, I'm here to take over the HF ranch.' Fenner saw a shadow cross Krone's large, expressive face and paused, but the man merely shook his head and turned away.

'I got to get your order out.' His powerful voice boomed in the close confines of the dining room. 'Remember what I said. For you, everything in here is free. Watch your back while you're in town.'

Fenner frowned as Krone returned to the kitchen. His gaze was upon Snark, now pushing himself into a sitting position and shaking his big head to clear cobwebs out of his brain. Snark's gaze came upon Fenner and he lurched to his feet, his expressison changing. He growled deep in his throat, like a bear awakening from hibernation, and his massive hands lifted, his fingers clenching and unclenching convulsively.

'Don't make two mistakes today, Snark,' Arlen called, and the town marshal's head jerked around on his solid neck until he was looking at the deputy sheriff. 'Get the hell outa here before I toss you in jail for disturbing the peace,' Arlen continued. 'I allus thought that one day you'd come up against someone like Fenner. It allus happens, and now it's caught up with you. You better shake hands with Fenner and admit he's the better man. Try your usual tricks and I reckon we'll have to plant you on Boot Hill.'

'The hell I will!' Snark shook his head and took a step towards Fenner's table, reaching out to pick up his pistol lying there.

'That would be the biggest mistake of your life,' Fenner said sharply. His right hand, lying on the table close to the gun, moved suggestively. 'You ain't wearing a badge so don't expect any favours. Try me again and you'll wind up dead.'

'I'll see you through gunsmoke for this,' Snark growled.

'I'll accommodate you any time – after I've eaten.' Fenner picked up the gun and emptied the cylinder, then tossed the weapon to Snark, who fumbled catching it. 'You'll need this, but don't come back tonight. The only thing I got on my mind right now is food, and I wouldn't wanta kill a man on an empty stomach. Now get outa here before I change my mind.'

Snark stuck his gun into its holster and turned away, his expression ugly. He departed, slamming the door so forcefully it almost sprang off its hinges. The tense atmosphere in the big room decreased. Fenner tried to relax but could not. He was not worried about Snark. He had come across town bullies before. But the way Krone's face had changed expression when the name Fenner was mentioned was something to remember.

'So you're a Fenner, huh?' Arlen had got to his feet and was on his way to the door but paused to talk. 'You're here to take over HF.'

'That's right. The ranch was left to me and my brother, who's with the herd we're bringing up from Texas. We plan to run cattle in Kansas. It will save trailing herds north.'

Arlen nodded. He was no more than thirty-five but youthful-looking, clean-cut. His manner was tough on account of his job, but Fenner noticed that the deputy's eyes were shifty, unable to remain steady while he was talking. Fenner felt a reservation creep into his mind and made a mental note to be careful around the man.

'I wish you luck.' Arlen nodded and departed.

Fenner relaxed a little and sat considering the situation until the waitress appeared from the kitchen with his order. She smiled wanly as she set a heaped plate before him, and Fenner sniffed appreciately as the smell of the food assailed his nostrils. He dropped his hat on to a neighbouring seat and prepared to eat.

'I'm Ruth Sheldon,' the waitress said, 'and I want to thank you for stepping in against Snark. Not many men would have done that.'

'Did he hurt you?' Fenner studied her face. She had a

washed-out look. There were lines on her forehead and wrinkles around her blue eyes, although he thought she could not be more than thirty and reckoned she was badly overworked.

She shook her head. 'It's not the first time Snark's pushed me around. Krone took him on the last time, and beat him good, but Snark hides behind his law badge. He enjoys picking on every stranger who rides in.'

'Maybe I've discouraged him from that habit,' Fenner observed. 'Although I doubt it.'

He began to eat but the waitress did not move away, and when he looked up enquiringly she moistened her lips and half-turned to leave, but suddenly slipped into the seat opposite.

'I owe you so I'm warning you about the situation in Brushwood,' she said hesitantly. 'You did me a big favour and it would be wrong of me to remain silent. May I talk while you eat?'

'Sure thing, but don't say anything that might get you into trouble later. I'm always ready for trouble, and I'd be surprised if there isn't a pile of it lying here waiting for me. My Uncle Henry was a hard man and I reckon he must have made a lot of enemies in his time, human nature being what it is. I guess I've inherited some of it with the ranch, and I've got to fight it or go under. There's no half way in this.'

'You're on the right track.' She nodded approvingly, then glanced around to see if she could be overheard. 'I hear plenty in here. Diners seem to think I'm part of the fittings and talk in front of me as if I'm deaf and blind. Some men in town are making plans to take over HF. They've been waiting for you to show up, and Snark has

13

been paid to kill you.' She laughed cynically. 'He sure found you too big a mouthful to swallow. It was a real pleasure seeing him get his comeuppance, but make up your mind to the fact that you'll have to kill him to stop him. He's been paid a hundred dollars to kill you. So you've got a real tough chore on hand and I don't think you can manage it alone.'

Fenner shook his head, his face set grimly. 'I ain't alone,' he responded. 'I got a brother and six cowpokes just two days from here, and I'd like to see the bunch that can face us down.'

'You're alone at the moment,' she said fiercely. 'Get out of town and stay away until your outfit arrives.'

'I appreciate the warning, but I got business here to settle tomorrow so the herd we've brought up from Texas can move straight in on HF.' His dark eyes glinted. 'No one is gonna run me out of town. I'm here to stay.' He paused and studied her intent face. 'You've done half the job,' he observed and saw enquiry fill her eyes. 'You've told me what the situation is, now give me the names of the men you overheard talking about it.'

'I told you Snark.' She glanced around again, and Fenner could see her tussling with her better judgement. 'They'd kill me if they thought I'd told you anything. You'll be making a call on Silas Hegg first thing tomorrow, I expect.'

'Hegg the lawyer. Yes.' Fenner nodded. 'He wrote me about Henry's death. What he didn't know and I didn't tell him was that Uncle Henry had sent us a copy of his will.'

'Hegg's name was mentioned when Snark was told to get you.' Ruth got to her feet. 'I've said too much already, but you've been warned, and there's little else I can tell you. Watch your back, that's all.'

'I'm mighty beholden to you, Ruth.' Fenner smiled. 'I know what it has taken you to tell me. If you do get any trouble through this then let me know and I'll handle it. If anyone threatens you then come on out to HF and tell me. Will you promise to do that?'

'Yes.' She smiled sadly. 'But you won't be on hand if they do decide to get me. I'll be dead by the time you hear about it.'

'You reckon it's that bad?' Fenner sighed heavily. 'I won't say a word to anyone that might give you away,' he promised. 'If Snark questions you, deny everything. Are there any honest men in town?'

'Some, but they would be foolish to stick their necks out for me. Brushwood is running scared, and it is difficult to tell who in town is honest.'

The food had been good – boiled beef and potatoes with all the trimmings. Fenner scraped his plate clean as she moved away. He gazed after her with a reflective light in his eyes as he mopped up his gravy with the bread that had been supplied. Getting to his feet, he picked up his hat, took a step towards the door, then paused. It was dark outside and Snark could be waiting in the shadows. Most of the other diners had departed while he was eating, and he went to the kitchen doorway and peered inside.

Ruth was washing dishes. Krone sat at a table eating supper, and he was talking in a remonstrative tone to the waitress, warning her against getting too friendly with Fenner. The big man arose at the sight of him, smiling regretfully.

'It has to be said,' Krone told him, shrugging his massive shoulders. 'There are dangerous men in

Brushwood who will stop at nothing to steal your ranch. Ruth has told you things she should not have mentioned. If word gets to the wrong ears then she will die.'

'I understand,' Fenner said quickly. 'I will act as if I didn't have the information. Nothing will be traced back to her.' He smiled. 'Don't let me interrupt you. I'd like to leave by the back door. I don't want to tangle with Snark again tonight and my guess is that he's out there in the shadows. I reckon to leave town now and return in the morning.'

He saw an expression of relief show briefly on Ruth's face. She began drying her hands.

'We're both on your side, as it happens.' Krone spoke bluntly. 'But people have been killed around here for not minding their business. You don't know what you're up against. The best thing you can do is go back to your herd and stay close to your men.' He paused and then grinned. 'There, you see, I warn Ruth against opening her mouth and fall into the same trap. Where will you stay? I got a spare room here if you're interested.'

'That's kind of you but it seems there is trouble riding at my shoulder. I'll head out of town and bed down where I can't be found. I've been sleeping rough for the past three months so it won't come as any hardship. Thanks for putting me on my guard. I reckon I can handle anything that comes up. See you around, huh?'

'Good luck,' Krone said.

'Be careful,' Ruth told him. 'My brother talked like you. He was afraid of nothing and wouldn't go along with the bad men, so they killed him.'

'He was the town mashal before Snark got the job,' Krone added, tight-lipped.

'I'm sorry.' It was clear to Fenner now why they had acted as they did. 'If its any comfort to you, I don't think Snark will last much longer. He's surely gonna take another bite at me.'

'And if you kill him you'll be a marked man,' Ruth told him. 'Then you won't have a chance.'

'I can only play the hand they deal me,' he retorted. 'So long.'

He crossed the kitchen and opened the back door, slipping outside quickly to press his back against the rear wall in the shadows while gazing intently around the back lots. A strong breeze blew into his face from the open range and he canted his head to pick up any unnatural sounds. The darkness was uncertain despite the thin crescent moon showing close to the eastern horizon and he waited for his eyes to become accustomed to the night. His right hand was down at his side, close to the butt of his pistol, and his nerves were hair-triggered as he readied himself for what he suspected was inevitable. He'd had no suspicion of trouble before riding into town but now it hung over him like a black cloud.

Long moments passed before he moved through the shadows like an animal, alert and dangerous. In his late teens he had ridden with the Texas Rangers for five years, learning grim lessons of the western way of life that were stamped indelibly in his mind. He had killed for the law, and was prepared to do so again for his own security.

He could not see to any great distance, and inched his way along the backs of the buildings fronting the street to get out of the immediate area of the eating house, half wishing that he had taken his brother's advice and travelled with a couple of their tough cowhands backing him.

17

He believed that any of them would be more than a match for the trouble building up in Brushwood. But he had always been a loner, and if this was his fight then he would attend to it on his own.

He turned into an alley that led back towards the street and moved slowly along it, almost feeling his way, having no intention of leaving town. No doubt his horse was being staked out now they knew he was in Brushwood, so he would not make the mistake of returning to the animal before morning. He reached the street end of the alley and craned forward to look around, realizing instantly that someone was standing on the sidewalk just beyond the corner. He caught the reek of tobacco, then heard a smothered cough, and froze in the act of stepping forward.

Fenner reached for his gun, the sound of it sliding out of its holster alerting the man, who came swinging round, uttering a cry of shock and fear. Fenner sensed the draw that accompanied the move and reached out with his left hand. He caught hold of a wrist as it lifted a gun from leather and twisted it away from his body. The man's gun exploded raucously, its muzzle flame a long ribbon of orange light in the shadows. The bullet crackled past Fenner's ear.

He stepped in close, gun in hand now, and swung the weapon in an arc, slamming the barrel against the man's head. He heard a smothered gasp as his pistol connected with a hat, and the man slumped to the ground, the echoes of the shot fading into the distance. He bent over the man, found him unconscious, and stepped back into the alley.

'What in hell are you shooting at, Charlie?' a voice

yelled from the shadows across the street. 'Ain't you got it into your thick head that there's to be no shooting? Say, have you shot someone, you jughead?'

Fenner eased away, moving back along the alley to the back lots. It seemed that a gun trap had been set up around the hash house and he needed to get out of it with no further trouble. He moved on along the back lots, wanting to get well clear. He could do nothing about his business until morning and, in view of the strength of the opposition against him, his best bet would be to fade into anonymity until the sun came up.

He had almost reached the far end of town before locating a barn on the back lots, and slid inside to take cover in a pile of straw. Despite the grim turn of events in his affairs, he was asleep within moments, and awakened in grey dawn light to find a youth standing over him with a raised pitchfork.

TWO

You near scared the life outa me, mister,' the youngster said, starting back a pace as Fenner reacted to his arrival by drawing his gun. 'What you doing in our barn? Are you the man everyone is all-fired up about – the one who busted Snark last night?'

'I guess I am.' Fenner holstered his gun with a slick movement. 'Who are you?'

'Jim Pardoe. Pa is the blacksmith. He was talking at breakfast about the man who bested Snark. I guess Snark picked on the wrong feller, huh? Pa said it was bound to happen.'

Fenner got to his feet and brushed himself down. 'Seems there were men on the street last night looking for me,' he said, 'so I snuck in here to wait for morning. Do you wanta to charge me for my bed?'

'Shucks, no, mister. Anyone who can lay Snark low is a friend of ours. Come on into the house. I reckon Pa will wanta give you breakfast.' The boy stuck his pitchfork into the pile of straw where Fenner had been sleeping and led the way out of the barn. 'Charlie Binns was hit on the street last night. He's in a bad way at the doc's place –

cracked head. Charlie is one of Snark's pards, and was watching for you.'

Fenner recalled the man he had bumped into at the alley mouth and heaved a sigh. He was getting caught up in minor incidents that could grow out of all proportion to the main problem he seemed to have inherited – a plot to steal HF. He followed Jim across a yard and into a single storey house fronting the street. In the kitchen a tall, heavily muscled man stood up from a table.

'I found this man sleeping in our barn, Pa,' Jim reported. 'He's the one put Snark down last night, and then laid into Charlie Binns. They're out looking for him this morning. I seen a couple of men lounging around the street armed with rifles.'

'I'm Travis Fenner, from Texas, bringing up a herd to take over the HF spread. Seems like I walked into a crooked scheme to take over the ranch.'

'Glad to know you, Fenner. I'm Jake Pardoe, town blacksmith. I knew your uncle well, and he was getting bad trouble before he died. He was a straight-shooter, and the wolves were closing in on him. He was being robbed blind before they finally murdered him.'

'Murdered?' Fenner's expression changed as shock filled him. 'I didn't know that. The report I got didn't mention murder. What happened?'

'Henry was found shot in the back out at Alder Creek. He had been in town on business and was going back to HF. There was an investigation. They never discovered the killer, but folks round here have a pretty good idea who was behind it.'

'Tell me,' Fenner urged.

'Sit down, have some breakfast, and I'll tell you what I

know. Like I said, Henry was a good friend to me – put a lot of work my way. He was a fine man and didn't deserve what happened to him. I heard him mention kin living in Texas. I wouldn't wanta steer you wrong, but you'll need to know the background of what's been happening round here.'

Fenner sat down at the table. There was a cold spot in his chest which had settled upon him at the news of his uncle's murder. It was obvious now that the plot to take over HF was bigger than he had imagined. He ate breakfast without really noting what was on the plate put before him, and waited impatiently for Jake Pardoe to start talking.

'Bear in mind that there's no proof to anything I tell you,' the blacksmith said. 'I got a pretty good idea that common talk is right on the nail, but don't accept it as gospel and go off half-cocked. You'll need to check out the details and get your proof. The talk is that Moses Quigley and his two boys are bossing the scheme to take over HF. The Quigleys run the Bar Q ranch west and north of HF. It's said that Moses used to be a rustler in the Big Bend country before he settled on this range, and it's true that rustling came in after he arrived. His two sons, Jake and Sarn, are a couple of hard cases who terrorize the whole county with their bullying ways. They sure gave your uncle a lot of trouble. It was like war was declared between the two ranches. It got so bad a couple of years ago that the Quigleys and their outfit were banned from town and had to go west over to Oak Ridge for supplies and the like. But that ain't stopped them causing trouble around here.'

Fenner was hard-faced as he listened. 'We never learned a thing about this or we'd have come up here with a big crew and handled the trouble for Uncle Henry,' he said. 'If I had known I wouldn't have ridden in alone. I'd have come loaded for bear. Heck, I walked in like a kid going into a candy store. I sure asked for what I got, and it's a wonder it didn't turn out worse. What is the law set-up around here? You don't need to tell me about Snark. I got him pegged to rights. I know Arlen is the deputy sheriff. He didn't seem to go along with Snark, but he sure as hell didn't ride herd on him last night. Is there a sheriff in town?'

'Nope. Sheriff Tooke is over in Oak Ridge, the county seat. He put Arlen in here because of the trouble, and Arlen has done a pretty good job so far. The men you've got to watch out for are Lou Jagger, Quigley's top gun, and Kane Tipple, who owns most of the business in town. Tipple started off buying the Mercantile and livery barn, but he owns just about everything except Al Krone's restaurant, and he's sure tried to run Krone out. As for Jagger, he's a killer, and there ain't anyone around here fast enough to stand against him. Jagger and Tipple are friends from Texas, and Jagger spends most of his time in town.'

'I've heard of Jagger,' Fenner said. 'He was mixed up in trouble along the Mexican Border a couple of years back. I'd left the Rangers then, but I got news of what was happening down there. Seems Jagger ran a big gang of rustlers until the Rangers cleaned them out. Jagger dropped out of circulation after that.'

'He's been around here about two years,' Pardoe said. 'Him and a dozen more like him, all branded with the same iron. They got a tight grip on the county. I think you'll need an army to make any impression on them. You sure won't get any help from the locals. Jagger has got them all running scared.'

'So that's the set-up.' Fenner rose. 'Thanks for breakfast. I've got some hard thinking to do. I need to see Hegg the lawyer to clean up a few details. Is there still a crew on HF?'

'Henry's crew was paid off after his death. Hegg took over the running of the spread, and brought in a tough bunch to handle it. You've got a fight on your hands, however you approach it.'

'I'll talk to Hegg first thing.' Fenner dropped a hand to the butt of his gun, his face hardening. 'I'll soon know if he ain't playing it square, and where I come from we know how to deal with shysters.'

'Don't go to Hegg's office after him,' Pardoe warned. 'He's got a gunhand covering him these days. The best thing to do is drop in on him at home, before he leaves for his office. His pet gunnie picks him up there just before nine, and after that he's never alone.'

'Where's his home?'

'Cross the street out front and make for the back lots over there. West Street cuts off to the right about halfway along Main Street. That's where the better houses are, and Hegg's place is the last house on the right – biggest place there is, with a white picket fence.'

'I'm obliged to you.' Fenner picked up his hat. 'Thanks. I'll be seeing you.'

'Any time,' Pardoe told him. 'It ain't my concern, but if I was you I'd postpone any business around here until I got some backing. The odds are long against you.'

Fenner nodded grimly and took his leave by the back door. He crossed the street and went to the back lots on

the far side, walking along the rear of the buildings until
he reached the road running west from the main street.
He paused under the shade of a tall oak and surveyed the
back of the big house before him. It looked like Hegg had
done himself proud. The building was two-storey and well
maintained. Easing his gunbelt, he drew his .45 and
checked the weapon carefully, then slid it back into
leather and pulled down the brim of his Stetson. He drew
a deep breath and strode resolutely to the back door of
the house.

The kitchen door stood ajar and Fenner pushed it open
gently and peered into a large kitchen. A middle-aged
man, dressed in a brown store suit, was seated at a large
table, eating breakfast and reading a newspaper. He was
short and fleshy, running to seed. His moon face was
pudgy, its outline blurred by fat, and his receding chin
seemed to have lost itself in the baggy flesh encompassing
his throat and neck. His long hair was very fair, almost
white, and his eyebrows were thick and bushy, startlingly
black.

Fenner stepped into the kitchen, his movement attract-
ing the man's attention. In the act of biting into a piece of
bread, he froze, his eyes widening as he gazed at Fenner
like a rabbit suddenly spotting a weasel. The piece of
bread fell from his pudgy fingers and he gulped on the
mouthful he had bitten off. His first attempt to speak
failed miserably and he gulped again, finally managing to
get his vocal cords working.

'Who in hell are you, walking into my house as if you
own it?' he demanded in a high-pitched tone. His face
had taken on an unhealthy pallor and his mouth gaped
open. He seemed inordinately scared, his hands trem-

bling so much he clasped them together as if he were praying.

'If you're Silas Hegg then I got business with you,' Fenner replied, closing the door at his back. 'I understand you're a mighty tough man to catch alone and my business won't wait.'

'I'm Hegg, but I don't handle business in my house at this time of the morning. I got an office on Main Street next to the bank. Come and see me there after ten. Now leave my house.'

'You sound like a man with a troubled conscience,' Fenner observed, 'and you're running scared. Maybe I'm the reason why you're nervous. I'm Travis Fenner. You wrote me a while back informing me that my uncle, Henry Fenner, was dead and had left the HF ranch to my brother and me. We're bringing up a herd from Texas, which is now resting on the town grazing ground at Twin Forks, and I need to clear up some details before it arrives on HF. I would have come to your office in the normal way, but when I got to town last evening I found a mess of trouble waiting, and learned that you and some others are in cahoots to take over HF illegally.'

'That is a scurrilous lie!' Hegg started to his feet but his legs seemed to fail him and he dropped back into his seat. His mouth opened and closed as if he were having trouble with his breathing. 'Who told you such a story? There is a deal of trouble in Clayton County but I am not involved. If you want the true version of what is afoot then talk to Arlen, the deputy. He'll put you straight.'

'You're not acting like an innocent man. When you wrote me why didn't you mention that Uncle Henry was murdered?'

'I told you he was dead, and that was sufficient to get you here.'

'You fired all the HF crew, I understand, and replaced them with hard cases.'

'The original crew were concerned about the trouble that had been hitting HF. They remained as long as they did out of loyalty for the brand, and quit when Henry Fenner was buried. I had to hire another crew to keep things under control out there.'

'I've got my own crew on the trail just two days from here so pay off your bunch and have them gone before my outfit arrives. If you are involved in some kind of a swindle then you better pass on the word that anyone trying something against my brand will wind up dead. Do you have any business to handle before I can move on to HF? Any papers to sign or the like? If so we'll go along to your office right now and get it done. I wanta head back to my outfit soon as I can and get loaded for bear.'

'There's no reason why you shouldn't take up residence without formality. I'll need you to sign documents, but that can be done later, after you've taken possession.'

'I can prove my identity.' Fenner drew his pistol and stuck the muzzle under Hegg's nose. 'Can you prove yourself? There is talk you're involved in bad dealing.'

Hegg leaned back in his seat to escape the muzzle of Fenner's gun, shaking his head violently in silent protest. His mouth was open but no sound issued from it. He was trembling, his eyes wide in fright. Fenner backed off suddenly.

'I reckon you get the message,' he said. 'Pull in your horns, mister. I'll do some checking up when I return with my outfit, and if I find a blemish on your record you'll be seeing me through gunsmoke. That goes for anyone else with ideas about taking over HF. Do I make myself clear?'

Hegg nodded emphatically. His fleshy face was ghastly pale. Fenner holstered his gun in a slick movement and turned to open the door at his back. He stepped outside, pulled the door to, and stiffened when a gun was stuck against his spine. He froze instantly.

'Who are you?' a voice demanded in his ear.

'What's it to you?' Fenner countered.

'Hegg doesn't do business outside of office hours. I'm his bodyguard.'

'What's he so scared of he has to employ someone to guard him?'

'He's got enemies, so I take care of his troubles. Open the door again and step inside. I wanta check you out.'

Fenner obeyed. He pushed open the door and stepped over the threshold. Hegg was still seated at the table, mopping his fleshy face with a white handkerchief.

'Who is this guy, Mr Hegg?' the gunman demanded.

Fenner spun around, his left elbow pushed out to catch the inside of the gunman's right wrist. His movement was so fast the man could not react before Fenner sledged his right fist against his jaw, simultaneously closing the fingers of his left hand over the man's gun hand and wrenching the weapon out of his grasp. The man fell to the floor and lay still.

Hegg was making whimpering sounds in his throat, like an animal caught in a trap. Fenner looked down at the bodyguard, a big man with all the earmarks of tough living imprinted on his features. His nose was badly misshapen and there was a thin white scar running diagonally across his left cheek from ear to nose.

'Not much of a bodyguard,' Fenner mused. 'What's his name, Hegg?'

'Deke Purdy. You won't get away with this, Fenner. I'll have the law on you.'

'Why? I dropped in for a business chat and this galoot made a bad mistake with his play. If it'll make you feel any easier, I'll report it to the deputy myself. I'm heading for the law office next and I'll tell Arlen about this incident. I might even bring a charge against Purdy.'

He unloaded the pistol and tossed it on the floor. For a moment he stood gazing at Hegg, but the lawyer would not meet his eyes. Fenner glanced at Purdy, who was beginning to stir, then departed. He walked to the main street and looked around, his hand close to the butt of his holstered gun. He was in a lot of trouble and did not underestimate the odds against him. It seemed that open season had been declared on him, but he would not run from trouble. Such an action was not in his nature.

He saw several men around the wide street, and a couple of them were toting rifles. The law office was two buildings away from the bank, and he crossed the street, walking quickly, reaching the door of the office just as it opened. Arlen stepped into the doorway. He was grinning.

'I saw you coming. You're making your presence felt in town. But you got a heck of a lot more trouble on your plate, Fenner. My best advice to you is get the hell out of town and don't come back until you've got your outfit backing you.'

'I'm riding out soon as I can, but no one is gonna run me out. I've got some business to settle. I heard this morning that my uncle was murdered – shot in the back. I gather he was having trouble before he was killed.'

'I'm sorry to say that is how he died.' Arlen's sharp features set into hard lines and his eyes glittered as he hooked a thumb in his gunbelt and leaned against a door jamb. 'I can't tell you much about it either. I sent for the sheriff soon as I got the word, and he made an investigation. Henry Fenner was the biggest rancher in the county and folks wanted to know what happened to him. But no one saw anything – leastways, no one came forward with information, and there were no clues to the killing.'

Fenner put a broad shoulder to an awning post and thumbed back the brim of his Stetson. His keen gaze raked the street but little was moving this early in the day. The sun was already hot and he could feel it burning the nape of his neck.

'HF was hit by rustling. Did you get a line on that?'

Arlen shook his head. 'I rode out several times but found nothing. There were some tracks but they disappeared in bad country to the north.'

'Do you have a map of the county?'

'Sure thing. Come into the office.' Arlen stepped back out of the doorway.

Fenner moved forward, and had one foot on the threshold of the office when a bullet splintered the door-jamb by his right ear. A six gun boomed from across the street at his back. He spun around, gun leaping into his hand, and saw a spurt of gunsmoke drifting from an alley opposite. The dark figure of a man showed in the shadows and, as the pistol fired again, Fenner dropped to one knee and triggered two quick shots, aware, as he did so, that a bullet which would have hit him in the centre of the body had he not dropped down, bored through the crown of his Stetson.

He squinted to pierce flaring gunsmoke and saw the figure across the street slam back against a wall as a result of his shooting, then topple forward on to its face. He got to his feet, breathing shallowly through his nose, and holstered his pistol.

Arlen pushed into the doorway, saw the downed man, and threw a glance at Fenner.

'Stay here,' he rapped, and went across the street at a run. The two men with rifles who had been watching the street were already converging on the spot. A dog appeared from the alley to sniff at the body. Arlen chased the animal away, then dropped to one knee beside the prostrate figure. He arose almost immediately and came back across the street.

Fenner remained motionless, watching the scene. The echoes of the shooting were fading away. Fenner's throat was raspy from inhaling gunsmoke. He glanced around the street and saw folks emerging from their doorways, attracted by the shooting. Ruth Sheldon and Al Krone came out from the hash house and stood on the sidewalk peering towards the grim scene. Krone was holding his shotgun. Fenner stepped out of the doorway on to the sidewalk to show himself and Krone waved a big hand.

'Who is the unlucky guy?' Fenner demanded when Arlen reached him.

'Deke Purdy, and he's dead. I'm wondering why he was gunning for you.'

Fenner explained his visit to Silas Hegg and Arlen nodded.

'That figures. Purdy was Hegg's strong-arm boy, and

always on the prod. Reckoned he had some kind of civil status, taking care of the lawyer. Him and Snark used to hang around together.'

'Where is Snark this morning?'

Arlen glanced quickly at Fenner's face, then nodded slowly. 'Funny you should ask that. I ain't seen him around, and its not like him to miss coming to the office. Mind you, he's something of a joke as the town marshal.'

'I didn't think he was funny when I met him last night,' Fenner responded. 'You sat at his table and let him get away with bullying that waitress. I rode with the Texas Rangers for five years, and not one of those men would have stood for anyone handling a woman.'

'I was about to step in but you beat me to it, and I could-n't have done a better job myself.' Arlen grinned. 'I'm seeing Thomas Benton this morning. He runs the bank and is the town mayor. I'm gonna suggest that he gives Snark his marching orders. The novelty of how Snark runs the local law has worn thin. Can I tell you anything else before you pull out?'

Fenner shook his head. 'I guess anything else can wait until I return with my outfit. I'd like to see your county map before I leave.'

'Sure thing.' Arlen led the way into the office and Fenner looked at the big map pinned to the wall behind the desk. 'That big area plumb in the middle is HF.' Arlen went behind the desk and lifted a hand. 'This is Q Bar to the north-west of you, and Circle C to the south-west. I don't know how you'll get on with the Quigleys – Moses Quigley and his two sons Sarn and Jake. They're mighty hard men, and they've sure caused trouble in the county.'

'I'll leave them alone if they leave me alone,' Fenner commented. He studied the map closely. 'My outfit is down near Twin Forks. I told them to hold the herd there until I get back to them. I can trail up this way, angling north and west, to hit HF on the southern boundary.' He impressed details of the range upon his memory. 'Thanks, Arlen. I'll be riding out now.'

'Keep your eyes skinned, just in case,' the deputy warned. 'Snark may be planning an unpleasant surprise for you.'

Fenner nodded and left the office. He went along the sidewalk towards the livery barn, taking his first look around Brushwood. The town was neat and clean. He looked into the general store from the doorway and liked what he saw but did not stop. He needed to look over HF before getting back to his herd and moving the outfit on to its new home range. As he passed the batwings of the saloon two men peered out at him. One of them thrust open the batwings. He was tall and slim, wearing a blue store suit and two guns on crossed cartridge belts. His eyes were a piercing blue. The other man wore a dark suit and a bow tie. Both men gazed intently at Fenner.

'What was the shooting about, stranger?' the two-gun man demanded.

'Some one called Deke Purdy got himself killed.'

'Did you kill him?' the other demanded.

'Yeah. He made a mistake and paid for it in full. Who are you?'

'Kane Tipple. What did you say your name is?'

'I didn't say. But it's no secret, and it'll be well known around here before I get much older. I'm Travis Fenner, one of the new owners of HF.' Fenner saw the two-gun man bristle at his name and asked, 'You got something on your mind, mister? Seems like my name touched you on a raw spot?'

'I'm Lou Jagger. No, you don't worry me, Fenner. I'm naturally interested in the man who's taking over the HF.'

'Hegg's bodyguard got curious about me,' Fenner retorted, 'and his curiosity killed him.' He went on along the street, looking to left and right, his hand close to the butt of his gun.

The barn was shadowy and Fenner entered cautiously, his hand close to the gun on his right thigh. He saddled up and checked his gear. Satisfied, he led the horse out front and permitted it to drink, watching his surroundings while he waited and liking what he saw. The town was quiet, but he reckoned there was much going on beneath the surface.

He was greatly disturbed by the news that his uncle had been murdered. Impatience was grabbing at him. He could not wait to start his own investigation into the events that had led to the violent death of a Fenner. If the herd had not been waiting he would have wasted no time getting on the trail of the unknown killers, for too much time had been wasted already.

His horse backed away from the trough, dribbling water into the thick dust. Fenner took up his trailing reins and stepped up into his saddle, and at that moment a figure stepped around the corner of the stable, sunlight glinting on the gun he was holding. Fenner caught the movement out of a corner of his eye and reacted instantly. He dived out of leather to his left, bringing the horse between the newcomer and himself, and hit the ground hard on his left shoulder. He rolled to the water trough and dived behind it, his pistol coming to hand. A shot crashed then, shattering the brooding silence, and a bullet thumped into the trough.

THREE

Fenner reared up from behind the trough, his gun ready. Shots were blasting furiously and gunsmoke obscured the front corner of the barn. His horse had run to the left, back into the barn out of the line of fire. Sweat trickled down Fenner's face. He threw up his gun and fired at the man peering through the cloud of gunsmoke at the stable corner. His pistol blasted twice in quick succession, the thunderclaps of the shots running into one. There was only the man's left shoulder and half his face showing at the corner but that was sufficient for Fenner. His first bullet smacked into the man's shoulder, the impact spinning him around and away from the corner.

Fenner remained watching, gun upraised, but held his fire when he saw the man's gun lying in the dust. The man sprawled sideways and fell upon his face to lie unmoving. Fenner kept low and checked the immediate area until he was satisfied the ambusher was alone. Then he got to his feet and stepped out of the half-inch stream of water curving out of a bullet hole in the side of the water trough.

Gun echoes were fading away, growling into the distance as Fenner glanced around, looking back along

36

the wide length of the street. He saw Arlen coming at a run along the sidewalk, followed more slowly by at least half a dozen men who had been attracted by the shooting. He turned on his heel and walked towards the downed man, who had not moved a muscle since hitting the dust.

The ambusher was lying on his face, a thin trickle of blood seeping into the sun-baked ground beneath him. Fenner bent and grasped a thick shoulder, pulling the man over on to his back. His eyes narrowed when he found himself looking into the fleshy features of Bud Snark. The town marshal was dead. Both Fenner's bullets had stuck home. One had bored through the big man's shoulder – the other had taken him through the throat. A town marshal badge glinted on Snark's shirt front.

Fenner backed off and stood waiting for Arlen to reach him. There was the reek of gunsmoke in the air and it sickened him, reminded him too much of the old days along the Mexican border – a time of much hard riding, fast shooting and death. Many of his fellow Rangers had given their lives for the sake of law and order. He sighed heavily and reloaded his gun, punching out the used shells and thumbing in fresh loads from his cartridge belt.

Arlen arrived, breathing heavily. He cursed at the sight of Snark spread-eagled in the dust. 'The damn fool!' he gasped. 'He didn't have enough sense to cross the street without help. He had to make his try, huh?' He looked at Fenner's hard-expressioned face, shaking his head as he considered. 'Well good riddance to trash. His days were numbered round here. I guess he tried his favourite trick once too often. You'll be back for the inquest, huh?'

'I reckon to be back in a few days.' Fenner spoke in a clipped tone. He was unmoved by the fact that he had killed two men in the space of scant minutes; men who lived by the gun and were merciless in their approach to the violent way of life they had chosen. He watched Arlen bend and snatch the law star from Snark's shirt, ripping the cloth.

'For the sake of the inquest,' Arlen said. 'I took this badge off Snark before he waylaid you. It'll make life that little bit easier for all of us. The cards are stacked against you, and after this there'll be very little I can do to help you. I'm on your side but I can act only according to the law, and the men you are up against don't step over the line. You got that?'

'I guess this is only the start of it,' Fenner mused, and Arlen nodded soberly.

Fenner went into the stable to find his horse standing in the stall where it had spent the night. He patted the restive animal, soothing it, then led it outside and swung into the saddle, lifting his right hand to his hatbrim as Arlen looked up at him. The deputy nodded and returned his salute. Fenner took the trail south. He rode at a canter until he was out of sight of the town then cut away right and rode northwest, making for HF range. He needed to check out the lie of the land before committing his herd to it.

He had a vague recollection in the back of his mind of visiting HF with his father when he had been about five years old. His father had recounted the visit several times afterwards, which had kept the memory alive, but Fenner reckoned that act alone could not account for the details which suddenly came into the forefront of his mind as he neared the big ranch some four hours later. When he reined in on a rise and looked down on the HF buildings from the distance of one hundred yards he recognized details that had been stored away in his memory since childhood.

A wide stream ran north to south through the valley housing HF headquarters. The ranch house was built solidly of timber with a front porch providing shade. There were a number of smaller buildings – bunkhouse, cook shack, store room, and a much larger barn in the background. Two pole corrals were off to the left.

Fenner let his gaze rove over the scene, recalling incidents that had occurred there almost a quarter of a century before, and an image of Uncle Henry loomed large and clear. He saw two horses in one of the corrals and another at the front of the house, tied to the porch rail. For long moments he sat gazing around, exercising his memory, and then touched spurs to his horse and rode down into the valley, mindful of the fact that the new crew here was in the pay of Silas Hegg, although their wages were drawn against the HF ranch account.

He followed the well worn trail, and was aware that he had been spotted long before he reached the yard. The gate had a notice nailed to it warning callers that they would be shot if they proceeded further. Fenner pulled the sign off the gate and discarded it, and by the time he had opened the gate and entered home ground there were three men standing on the porch. He held his reins in his left hand as he continued up to the house, his right hand lying easily on his right thigh within reach of his deadly gun.

He reined in a couple of yards from the house and sat his horse, returning the impassive gazes directed at him by the trio of range-clad men. They were of a class he would not have hired. Merely by looking at them he could tell they were more accustomed to handling guns than lariats. Their gun hands were close to holstered weapons, and one of them was carrying a Winchester, its butt tucked under his right arm, the muzzle apparenttly pointing at the dirt just in front of the porch but certainly covering Fenner's big figure.

'Who in hell are you, mister?' demanded the man with the rifle. 'You come in here like you own the place. Can't you read, or didn't you see the notice on the gate?'

'I am the owner,' Fenner replied. 'Travis Fenner. You got ten minutes to pack your gear and get off the place. I'm bringing in my own outfit and a herd of two thousand steers.'

'We was hired by Silas Hegg, the lawyer in Brushwood. He does the hiring and firing.'

'That was yesterday. I took over this morning, and I do my own hiring and firing. When you leave go into town and see Hegg for your wages. He'll settle up with you, and that will be the last chore he does for HF.'

'So you're a Fenner, huh?' The man with the rifle eased the long weapon, lifting the muzzle slightly.

'That's right. Get your gear now and pull out.'

'Well now, that ain't the way of it.' The muzzle of the rifle lifted an inch or two higher. 'I remember Hegg saying we should stay put no matter what happens. He wouldn't like us to pull out on the say-so of a stranger who turned up claiming he was the owner. We wouldn't be earning our pay if we didn't ask questions.'

'I tangled with Hegg early this morning, and had to kill his bodyguard to prove my point. Hegg is out of it now, and that goes for everyone he hired.'

BLOOD AND GRASS

'That's tough.' The man shifted his feet, then jerked up
the rifle quickly, his movement sparking his two compan-
ions into action. They moved apart, reaching for their
pistols. Fenner had read the signs of coming action and
his anticipation put him slightly ahead with his play. His
pistol came to hand smoothly, and was cocked and levelled
in a flash. He saw that the man with the rifle had no intention of stopping its movement upwards and triggered a
shot that smacked into the fellow's chest an inch above the
breastbone. The heavy detonation threw shock waves
across the porch and harsh echoes fled away across the
ranch. Fenner swung his barrel to cover the others as the
man fell back against the front wall of the house then slid
to the boards.

The other two froze when the shot blasted. One was
holding his six gun half-drawn. The other, slightly faster,
had cleared leather but his muzzle was still pointing at the
boards. He opened his fingers and the gun thudded
sullenly on the porch. The other thrust his pistol back into
its holster and lifted his hands well clear of his waist.

'OK, you tried to earn your wages,' Fenner said harshly.
'I'll tell Hegg so when I see him again. Dump your pistol,
mister, before you get another urge to use it.' He waited
until the gunman had complied. 'Now get out, and take
your pard with you. Get out, and fast.'

Both men came to life. They seized hold of their dead
gun pard, carried him off the porch, and threw his body
across the saddle of the horse hitched to the rail. One of
them led the animal as they crossed the yard to the corral,
and Fenner remained where he was, watching their move-
ments. They saddled up and rode out at a canter, leading
the burdened horse, and one of them even closed the gate

41

behind them. Fenner watched them pounding the trail towards town.

A movement at the cook shack attracted his gaze and he lifted his gun, then paused. An oldish man was standing in the doorway, watching him closely. He seemed to be unarmed, and Fenner stepped off the porch and walked towards him, disturbing the dust of the yard with his firm stride. As he neared the shack he narrowed his eyes against the glare of the sun, gazing intently at the oldster, feeling certain they had met before. The man was short and fat, his greying hair close to his skull in tight curls. He looked at least seventy, with a crooked nose and a mouth that lifted at one corner when he grinned, which he did as Fenner approached him. He came forward out of the doorway, limping badly, favouring his right leg and wiping his hands on an off-white apron.

'You don't need any introduction,' the oldster observed. 'Heck if you ain't the spitting image of Joe Fenner in his twenties. You must be Travis, huh? I'd a known you anywhere. Dang near twenty-five years ago when I last set eyes on you, a sprig of a lad then, and I used to dandle you on my knee. You sure look like a Fenner.'

'I'm Travis,' Fenner agreed, 'and don't tell me your name. It's coming back to me. Curly Brennan. My pa was always talking about you. He sent you north with Uncle Henry to keep an eye on him when he started this ranch.'

'He sure did, and I been here ever since. Was doing all right until I broke my leg and couldn't ride no more. Your uncle was short a cook at that time so I took over, and I been slinging hash ever since.'

Fenner holstered his gun and held out his hand. They shook hands warmly. Brennan was medium-sized, and had to tilt back his head to look up into Fenner's face. He had brown eyes that glistened in the sunlight and a face that reflected a cheerful manner, although his lips were pulled tight now and a scowl had narrowed his eyes.

'You come at a mighty bad time, Travis.' Brennan shook his head sorrowfully. 'Danged if I know how to tell you all that's been going on.'

'I learned this morning that Uncle Henry was murdered,' Fenner said. 'Can you throw any light on what happened? HF has been getting trouble, I hear. Who was back of it? And how come Hegg let you stay on here when he fired the rest of the crew?'

'Hegg didn't know I stayed on. Those hard cases he hired told me to stick around to do their cooking. I agreed, knowing you'd be coming up from Texas. Ain't you got a brother?'

'Sure thing. Albie. He's twenty-two now. Him and the Texas outfit are holding our herd at Twin Forks to rest up while I'm here getting the lie of the land.' Fenner went on to explain the incidents that had occurred since his arrival in Brushwood and Brennan's eyes gleamed.

'Heck, I would have gived a year's pay to see you kill Snark,' he said. 'That polecat needed putting down badly, and Deke Purdy. They're all part of the bunch that was brought into the county to take over HF. I've been keeping my eyes and ears open. It was easy to see Hegg was crooked and couldn't wait to get his snout in the trough. I reckon he teamed up with Q Bar. Moses Quigley and his two sons have had their eyes on this place for ever since they came into the county. And there are some in town you've got to watch. Kane Tipple and that two-gun smokeroo Lou Jagger. You've chased off those gunnies who were in the house, but there are more of them on the range, put here by Hegg to watch the spread, and they'll be back before sundown. What are you gonna do about them?'

'They'll get the same treatment as their pards.' Fenner drew his gun and reloaded the spent chambers.

'I heard tell you rode with the Rangers before you was full-growed. That sure is an outfit to teach a man how to handle himself. Me and your pa talked of joining them in our day, but Joe went into ranching and I stuck with him. I spent my life working for the Fenners, and a man couldn't have asked for better pards. I've been sore tried by Henry's death – shot in the back and nothing to point to the killer. I sure hope you're gonna poke around for sign now you're here, Travis, and let me side you while you're doing it.'

'I'll get round to it, you can bet.' Fenner heard the sudden rapid beat of approaching hoofs and turned quickly to see a trio of riders coming into the yard. 'Who are they, Curly? he demanded.

'Bad trouble in the flesh. That's Moses Quigley and his sons, Sarn and Jake. I'll get my shotgun. Don't give them half a chance, Travis. They're real mean right through to the marrow and poisonous as a bunch of rattlers. They've been banned from Brushwood but that don't stop them ruling the roost. Watch out for them, son. They'll be on the prod for trouble. I've never seen them when they ain't been wanting to gutshoot someone.'

Fenner nodded and straightened, mentally prepared for action.

Brennan leaned through the doorway of the shack and reached a hand inside to pick up a double-barrelled twelve gauge Greener leaning against the wall. He checked the weapon and tucked the butt under his arm, then leaned his left shoulder against a door post and faced the oncoming riders. Fenner moved slightly to the left and stood motionless, feet apart and right hand down at his side. The butt of his holstered pistol was touching the inside of his wrist. He narrowed his eyes slightly against the glare of the sun and waited patiently for the trio to arrive.

Moses Quigley rode ahead of his two sons, sitting astride a big white stallion, a massive figure weighing close to three hundred pounds, Fenner judged. He seemed squat in the saddle, looking as wide as a barn. Everything about him was outsize. He was dressed in a brown store suit that strained at every seam, and a flat-brimmed plains hat was pulled low over his dark eyes. His over-large face, with its layers of fat, was dominated by thick eyebrows that looked as if they had been painted on. His nose was long and broad, bisecting his face and overhanging a thin slit of a mouth that appeared to have no lips and looked mean.

He came towards the cook shack at a canter, controlling his mount with monstrous hands filled with brute strength. Fenner frowned as he watched the advance, which was a ceaseless battle for supremacy between man and horse. He let his gaze slide to the two following riders and his frown deepened. Sarn and Jake Quigley were twins, small by comparison with their father but each bigger than Fenner himself. They were dressed in good quality range clothes and bestrode identical chestnut horses. Both wore twin pistols on cartridge belts filled with glinting shells. Their heavy faces were set in grim lines as they came on, and they moved out to flank and cover their father as they arrived before Fenner and Brennan. They reined in abruptly, their hands close to their holstered guns, filled with an intentness which warned Fenner they were ready to fight at the drop of a hat.

'What in hell is going on here?' Moses demanded in a voice that sounded like a shovelful of gravel rolling around in a barrel. 'We just seen three of your crew riding to town, and Rafe Johnson was dead across his saddle.'

'What's it to you?' Fenner demanded. 'What happens on this spread is my business, and I don't like neighbours who come sticking their noses into what don't concern them. Hold it,' he added as one of the younger men started to dismount. 'Where I come from a man don't get off his horse until he's invited. So you're Q Bar, huh? I heard about you making big tracks on this range, and the way you rode in it figures you mean to ride roughshod over me. Well, you better change your minds as of now. I don't give an inch, and if you have a notion to take over this spread then you can start the wagon rolling by making your play right now.'

Moses Quigley made a big show of controlling his horse, but in reality he made the animal cavort and buck. The stallion snorted and stamped, raising dust with its restive hoofs. Fenner waited patiently until the animal settled down again.

'You got the look of a Fenner about you,' Moses rasped. 'It's about time you showed up. This range is under attack by a bunch of rustlers, and me and my boys are the only ones with the sand to stand up to them. We've been keeping an eye on this place like good neighbours, sticking out our necks, and you show up ready to bite the hand that's been fighting your battle.'

'That ain't the way I heard it.' Fenner smiled. 'And

there ain't no smoke without fire. If you are on the level then I'll apologize when I get to the truth. Until then you better stay clear of HF range.'

'I don't blame you for being suspicious,' Moses growled. 'You won't have many friends around here, but you'll soon see how the wind blows. I wish you luck – you're gonna need it.'

'You gonna let him talk to you like that, Pa?' one of the younger men demanded in a voice that rumbled deep in his massive chest. 'He's asking to be slapped around. Say the word and I'll get down and do it. If word gets out that you let a two-bit Johnny-come-lately stand up to you without getting his comeuppance you'll be opening the gate for others to try it.'

'Get off that horse and you'll need help getting back on it,' Fenner rasped. His stance did not change but an atmosphere of menace suddenly surrounded him. 'What's your name?'

'He's Jake,' Brennan said harshly. 'The other one is Sarn.'

'Who's pulling your rope, Brennan?' Jake demanded.

'I'm ready to stand up and be counted now there's another Fenner on the place,' Curly Brennan replied grimly. 'Somehow I get the feeling you Quigleys will have to pull in your horns after this. Its been a long time coming, but if you can't see it then you'll learn it the hard way.'

'That'll do,' Moses declared. 'I came to talk to you about the rustling, Fenner. We've got to get together to fight it. But we'll see you again when you've had a chance to settle in. I guess I don't blame you for your attitude. You'll soon learn who you can trust. Come on, boys.'

He whirled his mount away and departed in a series of bounds and leaps, fighting to control the spirited animal. His sons sat for a moment longer, gazing at Fenner with defiance on their harsh faces.

'You've got an almighty big mouth on you, Fenner,' Jake snarled. 'You better watch out in future. The next time you talk to Pa like you did I'll get real personal and teach you some manners.'

'Why wait?' Fenner responded, and there was a naked challenge in his harsh tone. He grinned when Jake threw a quick glance at his departing father. 'You can't make up your own mind, huh?' he baited. 'You need the old man's say-so. Well that figures.'

Jake growled and started his hand towards his gun butt. Sarn uttered a protest, but followed suit. Both Quigleys made a fast draw but halted before they could level their weapons for they were looking into the steady muzzle of Fenner's pistol, its black eye seeming to grow larger and more ominous with each passing second.

'Wowee!' screeched Curly Brennan. 'That was some draw, Travis!'

'Finish your draw, both of you,' Fenner instructed. 'You're on the brink so do it slow. I got an almighty nervous trigger finger when I'm facing your brand of pole-cat, and I don't need much encouragement at the best of times.' He paused and grinned. 'Unless you'd like to start over, huh? Holster your hoglegs and I'll do the same. Curly can count to three and we'll see if it comes out differently next time.'

Sarn Quigley opened his hand and allowed his pistol to fall into the dust. 'Do like he says, Jake,' he snarled. 'We'll come up with him later.'

'When you're behind me?' Fenner demanded. 'The way Henry Fenner was downed?'

Jake threw his gun to the ground and whirled his horse away. Sarn followed him closely. Moses Quigley was sitting his fractious mount by the gate, looking back towards the cook shack. Fenner heaved a sigh and holstered his gun. He was sweating and his hands were clammy.

'So they are the Quigleys, huh? Always on the prod. I got a feeling I'm gonna see a lot more of them in future. What do you know about them, Curly?'

'No one has ever proved anything against them. Both Jake and Sarn have killed men. Jake delights in doing it with his bare hands. He's the worst of the two, if that's possible. Moses once beat a man to death in the main street of Brushwood just for the hell of it. He was charged, but they trumped up the evidence and scared off witnesses. You got a tough fight on your hands, Travis. I sure hope that outfit you got coming up from Texas is man enough to handle the chore you're gonna toss into their laps.'

'What happened to the crew who rode for Uncle Henry? Hegg said he fired them. Did they stay around?'

'They was run out of the county, more like,' Brennan replied. 'None of the local ranchers dared take them on. They was a good crew, but there are professional gunnies on the range now, and before long you're gonna come up against Lou Jagger. He's top gun for the Quigleys, though why they need him I'll never know. Jake and Sarn can scare the kids when they're on the prod. You're gonna have to make a plan if you hope to beat that bunch, Travis. I guess they'll send Jagger for you, and he'll pick his time and place to get the drop on you.'

'I met Jagger in town just before I rode out. He was with Tipple at the saloon. I'm heading back to my herd soon as I've settled the rest of the bunch Hegg put in here. Maybe you better come with me, Curly. You stood up to the Quigleys with a gun in your hand, and I reckon you've put yourself in bad with them. I don't want to get back here and find you dead.'

'I ain't leaving here. I couldn't sit a horse, anyway. They ain't gonna run me out. I'll keep an eye on the place until you get back. As for facing down the rest of Hegg's crew, you ain't got to wait long. There are five of them coming in now, and by the looks of it they're loaded for bear.'

Fenner glanced towards the gate and saw a bunch of riders coming in fast. One man opened the gate for the others and they spread out into a ragged line as they came towards the cook shack. Fenner checked his gun and then holstered the weapon. He stood motionless, eyes narrowed, his gun hand seemingly inert at his side, but he was like a coiled snake inside and just as deadly, ready to strike if the situation boiled over into action.

Curly Brennan took a fresh grip on his shotgun and moved out of the doorway of the shack. 'If they start shooting I'll take them from the right, Travis,' he said. 'That OK by you?'

'Sure thing,' Fenner replied.

'And we shoot to kill,' Curly insisted.

The riders came on at a gallop, sunlight glinting on drawn guns. The next instant shooting started and, as hot lead smacked into the front of the cook shack, Fenner palmed his gun and dropped to one knee. Gun thunder rolled and echoed as he triggered his deadly weapon.

FOUR

Fenner did not seem to aim his shots. He pointed his muzzle at the rider on the left and squeezed the trigger, then shifted his aim as the man reared back in his saddle. He heard the boom of Brennan's shotgun as he covered a second rider and fired. The big Colt jerked in his hand and gunsmoke flared. Heavy echoes hammered away to the valley rim. His second man went down, and then it was over. All the riders were down, as were two horses, caught by the whirling loads of buckshot Brennan had fired.

There was a silent protest in the back of Fenner's mind as he pushed himself upright, fingers busy reloading his smoking pistol. His narrowed gaze swept around the yard and he saw the rider who had paused to open the gate now riding hell-for-leather back the way he had come. He yawned to rid his ears of the deafening reports of gunfire and thrust his pistol back into its holster.

'Check these men, Curly, and do what you can for them if they haven't cashed their chips. I'm going after that one getting away. I wanta know why they came in on the prod. Someone must have warned them I was here.'

'The Quigleys?' Brennan looked up from reloading his

shotgun. 'That's about their stamp.' He turned and studied the valley. 'I reckon they're out there now, watching to see what happened. Be careful, Travis. You could ride into more trouble than even you can handle.'

'That'll be the day.' Fenner drew his gun again and went forward to check the two fallen horses. One was dead. The other had a great wound in its chest. Its rolling eyes turned to Fenner as he levelled his pistol. He put a shot into its brain, watching as the animal threshed its hoofs in death. He continued to watch until the staring eyes dulled.

A sigh gusted through him as he went back to the porch of the house for his horse tethered there. He swung into the saddle and rode out, passing through the gateway and lifting the animal into a gallop. He could see the escaping rider, now far ahead, following the well-worn trail out of the valley. A shot echoed, and Fenner frowned when the rider threw up his arms and pitched out of his saddle. He looked around for the ambusher and saw a wisp of gunsmoke drifting from a spot under a cottonwood marking the edge of the stream flowing south.

Slowing his mount, he continued until he reached the downed rider, whose horse was grazing peacefully on lush bunchgrass. Stepping down from his saddle and covering himself by his horse, he subjected the line of trees, some two hundred yards away, to a searching gaze but saw nothing moving. When he was satisfied that the ambusher had pulled out he checked the fallen man to find him dead.

Fenner loaded the body across the saddle of the horse and returned to the ranch, leading the burdened horse. Brennan had been busy in his short absence. The four dead riders were no longer visible, and Brennan grinned harshly as Fenner dismounted.

'Those four are dead,' he reported. 'I dragged them behind the cookshack. They was spoiling the view out front. I heard the shot. You got the other one, huh?'

'Not me.' Fenner explained what had happened and Brennan shrugged.

'One of the Quigleys, I reckon,' he said firmly. 'They didn't want you to get hold of someone who might spill the beans about them.'

'I'll go into that later.' Fenner looked around. 'Cover the dead men and leave them. I'll have to ride into town again and talk to the law. I'll send the undertaker out here, then look up Hegg. He's got a lot of explaining to do. Will you be OK alone? There's no telling what will happen next.'

'I'll manage.' Brennan nodded. 'No one is gonna run me outa here. I'll keep an eye on the place. Watch your step, Travis.'

Fenner looked around. 'I don't see any remounts around,' he observed. 'Hegg hasn't kept the place up to scratch.'

'The ranch has been badly run down. I don't know what was in Hegg's mind when he did it. I guess you can take this horse when I get the body off. He sure ain't gonna ride it again.' Curly paused and glanced at the brand on the animal's rump. 'Say, this is a Circle C horse.' He dragged the body off the saddle and turned it face upwards. 'He ain't one of the men Hegg put in here and he ain't Circle C either. What was he doing with the other four, and how did he come by the horse? I heard Circle C lost some steers a couple of weeks ago. Mebbe the horse got took at the same time. It looks like this guy is tied in with the stealing, huh?'

'We'll check it out when I get the time,' Fenner replied. 'I'll shift my gear to this horse. It looks a lot fresher than mine.'

'I'll do it for you,' Brennan volunteered. 'Do you wanta eat before you ride?'

'No thanks, but coffee would be fine,' Fenner observed.

'There's a fresh pot on the stove. Help yourself while I take care of the horses.'

Fenner went into the cook shack. His thoughts were troubled. He had not expected any trouble around here, and now he was neck deep in it. He helped himself to a mug of coffee, anxious to get moving. His thoughts were deep as he considered the situation. He had a good idea now who might be handling the trouble, but proving it would be a horse of a different colour. He was keen to get back to his herd and bring it on to HF range, but needed to clear away some of the tangle surrounding the trouble before risking his stock in a place that was rife with rustling.

Brennan came into the shack and helped himself to coffee. 'The Circle C horse is ready for travel, he said.

'Who owns Circle C?' Fenner queried.

'Harvey Crench. I reckon he's a straight guy. His spread is off to the south-west. You'll get along well with Crench, I'm thinking. You have something in common with him. He's been hard hit by rustlers.'

'And so have the Quigleys, huh?'

'If you can believe them.' Brennan shook his head. 'I ain't never met a man on this range who would even think about stealing from Q Bar let alone going out to do it.'

'I'd better get moving. I'll take my horse along and

change back to it when I hit Brushwood. I'll leave the Circle C mount at the livery barn.'

Brennan grinned. 'I figured that. Just watch your step is all I ask. Your quickest way back to town is to follow the trail south.'

Fenner took his leave and rode south, leading his horse. The animal had carried him several hundred miles up from Texas along the Chisholm trail and was in need of a good of graining and plenty of rest. He had not reckoned to be riding around half of Kansas trying to sort out trouble. He had planned a quick trip ahead of his herd to smooth out any problems of inheritance before moving his beef on to home range.

He rode steadily, keeping a close watch on his surroundings. The heat blazed down from a cloudless sky and a haze brought indistinctness to the limits of his vision. He glanced along his back trail many times, bothered by a cold sensation between his shoulder blades that indicated someone was following him, but although he checked regularly he saw no signs of being shadowed. By mid-afternoon he was sitting on a ridge and looking down at Brushwood, and his thoughts were troubled as he followed the trail down to the huddled buildings straggling along either side of the wide, rutted street.

There were few people on the street, but Fenner kept his hand close to the butt of his gun as he dismounted at the hitching rail in front of the law office and tethered the two horses. He stretched tiredly, wishing the trouble was over but knowing instinctively that it had hardly begun. He entered the office to find the deputy sheriff dozing behind his desk. Arlen stirred at his entrance, and then got to his feet, wide awake in an instant. The deputy rubbed his eyes, grinning.

'I didn't get much sleep last night,' he apologized. 'I thought you'd be well on your way back to your herd by now. The town has been pretty quiet since you left this morning.'

'I needed to check out HF before fetching in the cattle.' Fenner described the incidents that had taken place out at the ranch and Arlen swore softly under his breath.

'So that's the way the land lies, huh?' he commented. 'I had a suspicion it might turn out like that when you showed up, but there was nothing I could do until things happened. I guess we both know who's likely to be at the back of this. Let's go talk to Silas Hegg.'

'I can't wait,' Fenner responded. 'Hegg has got a lot to answer for.'

Arlen led the way out to the street and Fenner explained how he had come to ride the Circle C horse. They reached the lawyer's office, and Arlen frowned when he found the door locked.

'That ain't like Hegg,' he muttered, and walked to the building next door. He entered, to emerge shortly with a grim expression on his face. 'From what I've heard I'd say Hegg has pulled stakes and split the breeze. Pete Darnell, the town carpenter, says he saw Hegg fetch his buggy, stop off at the bank, then head north out of town. He's been gone four hours. Let's go along to the bank. We should get a slant on Hegg's intentions from Tom Benton.'

Fenner made no comment as they went along the sidewalk. They entered the bank and Arlen pushed through a low gate in a polished wooden fence and walked to a desk set by the window overlooking the street. Fenner followed closely, and watched as the deputy spoke to a large, middle-aged man who was busy poring over a sheaf of papers.

'Tom Benton, Travis Fenner,' Arlen introduced. 'Fenner is the new owner of HF, Tom. You've been expecting him to show up for some time, huh?'

The banker got to his feet immediately, hand outstretched, and Fenner shook hands.

'I'm pleased to know you.' Benton's fleshy face creased into a smile. He was about fifty, his big moustache concealing the line of his upper lip, but Fenner could see tight lines around the mouth. 'I can see the Fenner family resemblance in you. I'm sorry you had to find this situation awaiting your arrival. Henry Fenner was a close friend, and I hope they get his killer.'

'You had a visit from Silas Hegg this morning, Tom,' Arlen cut in. 'Got any idea where he's gone? He left in a hurry and ain't been seen since he paid you a visit.'

'I've been mighty perplexed by Hegg's behaviour,' Benton said worriedly. 'He came bustling in here like the town was on fire, gabbling something about having to go to Ellsworth on important business. He closed his accounts here, saying he might not be coming back. I didn't know what to make of it, but he was at liberty to withdraw his money. I heard his bodyguard was killed this morning, and Hegg seemed scared and highly nervous.'

'He handled the HF ranch accounts,' Fenner said pointedly.

'He was your uncle's attorney, and handled everything pertaining to the ranch after Henry was killed. I can assure you that the account is in good order.'

'Hegg couldn't close the ranch account?' Arlen queried.

Benton shook his head. 'I supervized every transaction. I didn't like the way the old HF crew was fired, and I took Hegg to do over the hard cases he hired in their place. But there was rustling on the range and Hegg said he needed tough men to handle it.'

Fenner explained what had happened when he rode into the HF ranch headquarters and Benton's worried frown deepened.

'You killed most of Hegg's crew?' he said in a shocked tone.

'That's the way it came out when the chips went down,' Fenner replied. 'The three on the porch reached for their irons when I told them my name like they were waiting for me to show up. I also met the Quigleys. They came riding in as if they had heard the shooting and wanted to see if I was dead. That trio sure look like bad medicine. I reckon I'm gonna get a lot of trouble from their direction.'

'They are bad news in anybody's language,' Arlen said. 'The sheriff had to ban them from Brushwood. Moses ain't so bad on his own, unless he's been drinking. Then he can be hell on wheels. It's when he rides with his sons that bad things start happening. If they've got their eyes on HF then you're gonna have to kill them to stop them, Fenner!'

'I already accepted that.' Fenner nodded. 'What can we do about Hegg?'

Arlen shrugged, his dark gaze unfathomable. 'Far as I can tell he ain't done nothing wrong. There's no law against a man drawing his dough outa the bank and riding off. Check through Hegg's recent dealings for HF, Tom, and see if you can find any irregularities in the ranch accounts. I don't expect you to find any because Hegg is too clever for that. But it's the only chance I got right now of pinning something on him. My hands are tied until the law is broken. Sorry I can't be more helpful, Fenner.'

'I know how the law works,' Fenner responded. 'I'll get around to Hegg later. Right now I better make tracks for my herd and get it pointed towards HF. When my crew is settled on the range I'll start taking on the trouble that's brewing.'

'I'm gonna ride out to Oak Ridge to see Sheriff Tooke,' Arlen said. 'He'll need to know how this situation is panning out. I don't have to warn you to be on your guard, do I?'

Fenner laughed harshly. 'I've been breathing gunsmoke ever since I hit this range,' he observed. 'I can sure see which way the wind is blowing. I'll drop in and see you later, Benton. I guess I'll be doing my business with you.'

'Glad to know you, and you can entrust your finances to me with every confidence,' the banker said.

When they returned to the street, Arlen paused and pointed to three riders outside the law office. They were taking a great deal of interest in the horse Fenner had ridden in.

'There's Harvey Crench now,' Arlen said. 'He's spotted the Circle C brand on the horse you rode in. Let's go talk to him. Crench only comes into town these days to report more cattle losses. The rustlers have near bled him dry. He's been breathing fire and brimstone for weeks, but can't get a sight of the thieves.'

They went back towards the jail. Fenner studied the tall figure of Harvey Crench. The Circle C rancher was well into his fifties, thin like a bean pole, and his taut features made him look like he was haunted by trouble. Arlen introduced them, and Crench nodded, his hand shake a mere formality.

'How'd my horse get into town?' he demanded.

Fenner explained, and Crench nodded.

'That animal was stole off my place last week. Where's the feller you said was riding it?'

'He's lying dead behind the cook shack on HF,' Fenner told him, and saw a glint of interest flare briefly in Crench's brown eyes.

'Did you make him talk before he died?' Crench asked.

Fenner explained the circumstances of the unknown man's death and the Circle C rancher nodded again.

'I'll drop by your place when I ride back to my ranch,' he said. 'I'd like to get a look at that guy. You got any idea who shot him?'

'No. It was an ambush shot from about two hundred yards. I didn't have time to check it out. I've got to get back to my herd. Once I've got my beef moved on to HF I'll be able to spend time hunting the rustlers.'

'There's more than rustlers on this range,' Crench said heavily. 'Three men rode into my place at dawn and fired about fifty shots into the buildings. They filled the place full of bullet holes. Scared the hell outa my wife. I sent a couple of men to try and track them down while I came on here to report it to you, Arlen. What are you gonna do about it? Or will it be the same as usual?'

'I'll drop into your place on my way to see the sheriff,' Arlen said. 'That's all I can do.'

'There ain't much help coming from the law in these parts,' Crench said sharply. 'Never has been. That's why we're getting all this trouble. Henry Fenner was dry-gulched and the law didn't find his killer. We better get together, Fenner, when you've got your herd settled, and see what we can turn up on these rustlers. If you don't keep a close watch on your cattle they'll disappear like every other herd around here. They're stealing us blind and nothing is being done about it.'

'All that will change when I get back,' Fenner said bluntly. 'I won't expect the law to step in and stop the rustling. Where I come from, a man fights his own trouble. I'll raise some hell myself when I'm ready.'

'You've been raising hell ever since you hit Brushwood,' Arlen observed.

'There's more than enough of it to go round,' Fenner commented. 'I'll put my gear back on my mount and you can have your horse back, Crench. It's time I trailed south again.'

In a few moments he was astride his horse. He lifted his hand in farewell to the men watching him and set off at a canter, but reined in to the sidewalk when he spotted Al Krone standing in the doorway of the hash house. The big man motioned for Fenner to join him, then turned and disappeared inside the building. Fenner tied his horse to the rail outside and followed Krone.

The rush hour had ended and the interior of the restaurant was spotless and strangely still. The odours from cooked food informed Fenner that he was hungry but he had no intention of stopping to eat. Krone was waiting by the kitchen door. Fenner could hear the sound of crockery being stacked somewhere in the background and wondered if Ruth Sheldon was still working.

'I need to talk to you.' Krone's face was set in harsh lines, his eyes filled with a brightness that seemed to

61

inflame his heavy features. 'I've been keeping an eye open for you. Something was said in here earlier that I reckon you should know about. Mack Tomlin was in around noon with another hard case. Ruth overheard them talking. Tomlin is a gunnie who hangs out around town. Someone is paying him, that's for sure, because he lives well and he ain't got a regular job. He was talking about a gun chore that's come up. Someone is gonna get it in the neck. No names were mentioned, but it sounded like you were being nominated, Ruth said. She was worried so I said I'd keep an eye open for you. Tomlin and the other guy went to the livery barn when they left here, and I watched them ride south when they pulled out minutes later.'

'Thanks for the warning.' Fenner dropped a hand to his holstered pistol. 'I reckon they'll be waiting for me along the trail. I should think everyone around here knows I'm heading south again. I'll keep my eyes lifting for them. Can you describe Tomlin?'

'Yeah, he's a short, muscular redhead. Wears a blue store suit and carries twin Colts on crossed cartridge belts under his jacket – looks like he's always ready to start a war. He rides a horse black as midnight. You'll know him if you set eyes on him.'

Fenner nodded and departed, swinging easily into his saddle, his gaze encompassing the street as he went on. When he reached the open trail he drew his Winchester from its scabbard and checked it. The knowledge that he might be a target for ambush keyed him up for what he would have to do, and there was a tight sensation in his chest as he cantered towards the distant town of Twin Forks.

Nightfall found him making camp in a gully. He moved

around casually although his body and nerves were attuned to the grim task of watching his surroundings. His ears were strained for unnatural sound and his right hand stayed close to his holstered pistol. He ate cold food and drank stale water from his canteen. Darkness fell quickly and he moved away from the campsite, sneaking like a wild animal through the dense shadows to settle down yards away from his knee-hobbled horse to begin a lonely vigil that took him through the night without incident. He was drowsing as the greyness of predawn crept over the land, but was ready saddled and moving out when the first rays of the sun showed above the horizon.

He expected trouble within the first mile and rode steadily, nerves hair-triggered, but nothing disturbed the silence and loneliness of the trail and he pushed on faster, staying off the trail, avoiding skylines and likely places of ambush. It was mid-afternoon when he spotted a trading post beside the trail, and two horses were standing hipshot at the rail outside the door. Fenner's eyes narrowed when he saw that one of the animals was black.

He eased back into cover, dismounted, and sneaked forward until he could study the trading post from a distance of about fifty yards. The place was silent and still. There was a pole corral off to the right, where three horses were being held. Fenner considered. He had no idea what lay before him. Perhaps Tomlin had met up with some more of his ilk and they were waiting here for him to ride in. He didn't need trouble now, he decided, although he was not a man to duck a fight if it had to be faced.

He went back to his horse and, as he swung into his saddle, a harsh voice called to him from behind:

'Hold it right there, mister, and throw up your hands.'

Fenner obeyed without hesitation and sat motionless in his saddle. He heard boots scuffing the hard ground and then a small man stepped into view from behind his left shoulder. The man was wearing a store suit. He had a long-barrelled pistol in his right hand and another in a holster on his left hip. Fenner saw signs of red hair under the brim of the man's hat.

'Mack Tomlin,' Fenner said through his teeth.

The man's grin disappeared. 'You know me from some-where?' he demanded.

'You were described to me before I left Brushwood. I've been expecting you to make a play for me.'

'Uhuh. You're Fenner, ain't you? They got your descrip-tion right. Big man from Texas. You've raised hell since you rode into town last evening. Killed Bud Snark and Deke Purdy, so I heard. That kind of thing don't go down well around here, so you're slated for Boot Hill. I reck-oned you'd play it cute and sneak up on the trading post, and I fooled you, huh? You saw my horse standing outside the post and figured I was inside. But better men than you have been fooled, and I got to beef you now.'

'Who paid you to kill me?' Fenner demanded.

Tomlin grinned. His face was thin and long, his eyes overbright and alert. 'It's a funny thing, but most men ask me that before I put their light out. As if the knowledge makes any difference at a time like this.'

'I got a good idea who's behind it.' Fenner spoke casu-ally, but he was coiled like a spring inside, ready to take advantage of the slightest lapse on the gunman's part. 'Silas Hegg is a frightened man. I killed his bodyguard, and Hegg lit out. He wants me out of the way before he goes back to Brushwood.'

Tomlin shook his head. 'You got the wrong man there, feller.'

A footstep sounded on the hard ground behind Tomlin, and Fenner saw a hard case approaching. Tomlin's gaze flickered and strayed from Fenner, but steadied immediately, and Fenner restrained his breathing. The footsteps drew closer, and Tomlin could not resist throwing a quick glance over his shoulder. Fenner dived to the ground, drawing his gun as he did so. Tomlin swung back to him, his gun blasting, and a bullet stung Fenner's left forearm as he hit the ground heavily.

Fenner fired instantly. The heavy reports of the shots blended into one and rolled away across the range. Tomlin was in the act of squeezing his trigger again when Fenner's slug took him in the centre of the chest. He lost all interest and flung his hands wide as a half-inch chunk of lead bored through his sternum and blasted into his heart.

Fenner rolled quickly, his gaze on the approaching man, who had halted as the shots reverberated and was now staring in disbelief at the scene before him. Fenner got up on one knee, his muzzle steady, covering the newcomer, who was too shocked to attempt to draw his holstered gun.

'Throw up your hands,' Fenner rasped, 'and be quick about it.'

The man obeyed, shaking his head in disbelief.

'You've killed Tomlin,' he gasped.

'And you're next on my list, if you ain't careful,' Fenner told him.

'Are you Travis Fenner? You look like the man Tomlin described.'

'Shut up and do some listening,' Fenner rapped. 'I'll ask the questions, and you'd better come across with the right answers. I know enough about the situation to tell if I get the truth or not.'

'I can't tell you anything.' The man kept his hands high.

'We'll see about that,' Fenner retorted. 'Get rid of your gun and do it slowly or you'll follow Tomlin clear into hell!'

FIVE

Fenner skirted the fallen Tomlin as his prisoner disarmed himself by lifting his pistol from his holster with finger and thumb and tossing it away. He pushed his hands high above his shoulders, evidently impressed by Fenner's gun skill. Fenner stepped in close, gun ready, and searched the man for other weapons. He moved back out of reach and holstered his pistol, glancing down at his left forearm to check the wound he had received. Blood was dripping from a superficial groove that had been caused by Tomlin's slug. He removed his bandanna, shook the dust out of it, and tied it tightly around his forearm.

'What's your name?' he demanded.

'Frank Eastoe.'

'Who paid Tomlin to lay for me?'

'I don't know, mister, and that's the truth. Tomlin looked me up in Brushwood and offered me ten dollars to ride with him today. Heck, we'd got here to the trading post before he told me what it was all about. He just wanted me along to watch his back while he attended to you. I didn't want the job when he told me about it, and he said he'd shoot me if I didn't go along with him.'

'What did you talk about on the ride from Brushwood? Tell me about the local set-up. I know much of what's going on so I'll be able to tell if you start lying. Play it straight with me and I might turn you loose. Lie to me and you'll wind up with a bullet where you can't digest it. Start by telling me what you do around Brushwood?'

'I ain't got a job right now.' Eastoe shrugged.

'What do you do when you are working?'

'I chase cows mostly.'

'A good puncher can always get a riding job,' Fenner observed. 'Are you workshy or just plain lazy?'

'Neither. I don't like the set-up on this range. There's bad trouble coming and I don't wanta get mixed up in it.'

'Bad trouble has arrived. Henry Fenner was killed with a shot in the back. It couldn't have got any worse than that for him. What do you know about his killing?'

'Nobody knows anything about it. Even the law can't find out who fired the shot.'

'If you're not working then where do you get your living money from? You can't freeload all the time.'

'I do odd jobs for folks.'

'Like this job you took with Tomlin, huh? You don't care what you have to do to earn a few dollars, is that it? Well you sure jumped in with both feet this time. You ain't told me a thing about what's going on around here, which proves that you're against me. I've a mind to take you along to where my herd is being held and turn my crew loose on you. They ain't had any fun since leaving Texas three months ago. I reckon they would just about eat you, guts and feathers. Who's in the trading post?'

'Just the trader and his wife.'

'What did Tomlin do around Brushwood? He's a

gunnie. I bet he never chased a cow in his life unless he
was rustling it.'

'He works for the bank. Most days he guards the place.'

'And gets time off to handle killing jobs, huh? Listen,
Eastoe, I'm gonna turn you loose. I got too much on my
plate to want you on my hands. Just bear in mind that if I
ever set eyes on you again I'll kill you. Fetch your horse
and split the breeze until you shake the dust of this range
off your boots. You got that?'

'Anything you say.' Eastoe nodded emphatically. 'I'll be
long gone by the time you get your herd to HF.'

'Beat it then, and don't look back.'

Eastoe nodded, turned abruptly, and hurried off in the
direction of the trading post. Fenner watched him until he
had covered at least half the distance, then went to his
horse and swung into the saddle. He rode on a detour,
deciding against visiting the post, and hit the trail beyond
it. From time to time he glanced along his back trail,
riding south until he spotted the lights of Twin Forks just
after the sun went down.

He skirted the town, making for the grazing ground
where his herd was being held. Night closed in and a faint
crescent moon showed in the east which pierced the
dense shadows with pale silvery light. He slowed the horse
to a walk when he was near to the cattle camp, and reined
in when he spotted the stark outline of the chuck wagon
silhouetted against the waxing moon.

'Hello the camp,' he called, and heard his voice echoing in the silence. 'Show yourself, Spare Rib. You better
not be drunk this early in the evening.'

He noticed then that there was no campfire, which
meant no meal being cooked. He stepped down from his

saddle and went to the wagon, his right hand on his gun butt. The shadows were dense on the ground. His right foot caught on something that was invisible to his narrowed eyes, and he sprawled heavily. Cursing, he pushed himself to his feet and fumbled in his breast pocket for a match, reaching out with his left hand for the lantern he knew was hanging just inside the wagon.

Lighting the lantern, he held it high and looked around. His gaze fell immediately on a figure that had tripped him. The rays of the lantern illuminated the stiff features of Spare Rib, the cook, who had a dark patch of blood on his shirt front. Fenner dropped to one knee and checked for signs of life, and a bitter sigh escaped him when he discovered that Spare Rib had been dead for several hours.

He straightened and held the lantern aloft to search the immediate area. Blanket rolls were dotted around in preparation for the night, but there was no sign of his crew. The campfire had been out for hours. No food had been cooked that day. Fenner walked farther afield, looking for his herd, and found no sign of it on the grazing ground. He returned to the body of the cook, his thoughts turning in a grim circle. The herd had stampeded or been run off and the crew were out after it. But how had Spare Rib died?

He crouched over the cook, holding the lantern high in his left hand, and peered into the familiar bearded features that somehow looked different set in death. He unfastened the blood-soaked shirt and peered intently at the man's chest. The yellow glare of the lantern revealed a neat round hole in the centre of Spare Rib's chest. Fenner sat back on his heels, fighting to control his shock.

He arose abruptly and turned to examine the wagon, his teeth clicking together when he spotted bullet holes in its side. The camp had been attacked. He went to his horse, swung into the saddle and, holding the lantern high, rode around in a wide circle, searching the area for more bodies. He found two dead horses but no sign of men, and finally returned to the wagon, unable to discover more than the bare fact that the herd had been run off.

There was nothing he could do until morning, when tracks in the dust might tell him the story of what had happened. He doused the lantern and returned to the wagon. As he dismounted, a harsh voice called to him from the blackness surrounding the vehicle.

'Lift your hands and stand still. I got a gun on you. Who are you and why are you skulking around here?'

'I'm Travis Fenner. This is my camp. I've just returned from Brushwood. Who are you?'

'Frank Lambert, deputy sheriff of Twin Forks. Light that lantern again so I can take a look at you. I been told what Travis Fenner looks like.'

'What happened here?' Fenner demanded.

'Light the lantern and then we'll talk.'

Fenner obeyed, and when yellow lantern-light flooded the area he caught the glint of a law star on the chest of the dark figure that came forward, gun in hand.

'Hold up the lantern so I can see your face,' Lambert commanded.

Fenner obeyed and was studied closely.

'I reckon you could be Travis Fenner,' Lambert observed, and holstered his gun. 'There's been hell to pay here. A bunch of men hit your herd last night. Three of

71

your crew were killed fighting the rustlers. One was bad wounded and is like to die, so Doc Harper says. He's your trail boss, Bill Blick, in town nursing bullet wounds. He said he was expecting you back from Brushwood any time so I've been keeping an eye open for you.'

'Who is the man bad wounded?' Fenner demanded.

'Your brother Albie. I'm sorry to be the bearer of such bad news, Fenner. Your three dead men are Santee, Forbes and Brewster. This is a real bad business, and then some. If you're ready to ride into Twin Forks I'll take you to the Doc's place, where your brother is being nursed.'

Fenner doused the lantern and went to his horse. He swung into the saddle and joined the deputy, who set off at a fast clip towards the lights of the nearby town.

'I sent a couple of men out to track the herd,' Lambert told him. 'They ain't returned yet. It sure is a bad business.'

Fenner pushed his horse into a gallop when they reached a trail going towards the town and the deputy stayed with him. They cantered through the town and Lambert reined up in front of a big house.

'This is the Doc's place, he said. 'Come on.'

They dismounted and approached the house. Lambert rapped on the door, which was half opened by a middle-aged woman holding up a lantern. She peered at them anxiously, half ready to flee, Fenner thought.

'Miz Harper, this is Travis Fenner whose herd was run off last night. It's his brother you're nursing.'

'Come in, Mr Fenner.' She opened the door wide, her tension fading. 'I can tell you your brother is making progress. My husband has been tending him constantly since he was brought in last night, and thinks he will pull through.'

'Thank you, ma'am.' Fenner glanced at the deputy as he entered the house. 'Is there an undertaker in town?'

'Sure is. Joss White.' Lambert was middle-aged, tall and thin, with a harsh face.

'Ask him to take care of the body of my cook out by the wagon, will you? I'll attend to the details later.'

'I'll take care of it.' Lambert departed, touching his hat brim to the doctor's wife.

Fenner entered the house and removed his hat as he followed the woman up a flight of stairs and into a room dimly lit by a single lamp. He paused in the doorway, looking at his brother stretched out in the single bed. A middle-aged man was seated on a chair beside the bed, drowsing as he maintained a vigil. He started up at the sound of the door opening, and held out a hand as Fenner entered. He was tall and thin, balding, with a pair of spectacles perched precariously on his nose.

'I can see that you and my patient are related,' he observed. 'I'm Doc Harper. Glad to meet you. There was a time when I thought you wouldn't get back to see your brother before he died, but he rallied a couple of hours ago and now he's likely to pull through.'

'Thanks, Doc. That is good news.' Fenner studied Albie's pale face, emotion tugging at him inside. 'Where was he hit?'

'In the chest. I extracted the bullet, and a piece of his shirt that was carried into the wound. We'll have to wait now to see if infection will set in, but I think he'll make it without trouble. Your trail boss is in a room at the hotel. He took two bullets but the wounds are not serious. He'll be up and about again in a week. I'm afraid your brother will take a lot longer to recover.'

'Can I leave him in your care?' Fenner asked. 'I'll pay whatever it costs to put him back on his feet. I'm gonna be real busy from tomorrow, hunting the rustlers. They killed three of my men – good punchers who were friends of long standing. I've got a big score to settle.'

'Your brother can stay here. He'll need constant nursing for a week or so. I have a good nurse who measures up to the job. Come and see me first thing in the morning. I should be able to tell you more by then.'

'Thanks, Doc.' Fenner gazed at Albie, shaking his head slowly as he tried to overcome his shock. 'I better start making plans for the morning. I'll see you before I ride out.'

'Call at any time,' Harper responded.

Fenner left and stood on the sidewalk outside the house to look around. There were lanterns along the street at spaced intervals, giving dim light to their surroundings. He saw the hotel almost opposite and led his horse across to the tie rail in front of the large building. His spurs tinkled as he crossed the sidewalk and entered the lobby.

The clerk showed great interest in him when he asked for the number of Bill Blick's room.

'I'll show you up myself,' he said.

'No need to,' Fenner countered. 'Are you taking good care of Blick?'

'He's getting the best treatment.'

'Make sure you give him the best. I'll pay whatever it costs. I'll need a room for tonight. Can I get some food in about twenty minutes? I haven't eaten all day.'

'Sure, if you'll take pot luck. Sign the register.' The clerk picked up a pen, dipped it in an ink pot and held it out for Fenner. 'Room Seven. Mr Blick is in Six. Will you want breakfast in the morning?'

'Sure.' Fenner booked in and took the key of his room. He ascended the stairs two at a time and thrust open the door of Room Six. Pausing on the threshold, he found himself looking down the barrel of Blick's unwavering pistol. 'You don't need that right now, Bill,' he said.

'Travis!' The hand holding the gun dropped to the bed and Blick slumped back wearily. A man in his forties, short and solidly built, he was stripped to the waist. His chest was heavily bandaged. He was wearing his Stetson, and yellow hair showed from under the wide brim. 'I'm sure glad to see you, Boss. Where in hell have you been? Hell busted out here.'

'I know about it,' Fenner entered the room and closed the door at his back. 'I've seen Albie. He doesn't look too good. I met Lambert, the deputy. He told me what happened.'

'We got took by surprise.' Blick's voice was harsh. 'Everything had been so quiet since you left. They came helling out of the night, spooked the herd and ran 'em off, shooting at everything that moved. I got two slugs in the chest, but the Doc reckons they ain't serious. I kept on my feet until I got Albie into town. But Spare Rib wasn't so lucky, and I heard this morning that three of the boys were killed chasing after the rustlers.'

'Albie is gonna be all right, so the Doc says.' Fenner nodded. 'I'll be heading out in the morning to trail the rustlers and collect from them for our riders.'

'Sure, and I'll ride with you. I've been resting up waiting for you to get back.'

'The hell you will. I want you to stick around here and keep an eye on Albie. I found a lot of trouble up in Brushwood. Someone is trying to take over Uncle Henry's spread. I was knee-deep in shooting most of yesterday. I've come back for my outfit, and find it's had the hell shot out of it.'

'It would have ended differently if I hadn't taken these slugs,' Blick said fiercely. 'And there was Albie. He was hit real bad. I thought he was dead when I turned him over. Thank God he's gonna make it. We got some fighting to do, Travis. I wish to hell I hadn't been shot. I need to be up and about. We got some paying back to do, and it don't seem right that I can't go along with you.'

'You ain't going so make the best of a bad job and rest up until you get back on your hind legs. I'll need you bad when we get the herd to Brushwood, Bill.'

Blick's fierce expression faded and he slumped in the bed. 'It's the helluva note,' he said heavily. 'I feel like I've let you down, Travis. But we didn't stand a chance. They were mighty slick, those rustlers. Seems to me they knew what they were doing.'

'They won't get away with it,' Fenner countered harshly. 'We can't bring back the dead, but we can sure as hell pay their bill for them. I'll nail every one of those thieving sons or die in the attempt.'

'I know how you feel, and I've been saying all along we shoulda brought a bigger crew, although I reckon a dozen hands wouldn't have been able to stop those rustlers.'

'I heard up in Brushwood that some of the men against us worked as rustlers down along the Mexican Border. I'll be looking them up soon as I get the herd back.'

'You can't go after those buzzards alone.' Blick shook his head helplessly.

'Is there anything you need?' Fenner moved to the door as he spoke. 'I got to eat before my ribs bust out through my skin, and I got things to do before morning. I'll be riding out at dawn, following sign. I'll get that herd back, unless those cows have sprouted wings and flown back to Texas.'

'I'll get on my feet tomorrow,' Blick promised. 'I'll take it easy until Albie is out of the wood. Why don't you hire a couple of local men to side you? It'll be wrong to ride out alone, and you dang well know it.'

'After what happened around Brushwood I don't feel like trusting anyone I don't know. I'll see you when I get back, Bill. I'm counting on you to do the right thing around here.'

'Yeah.' Blick turned his face away and Fenner departed to take care of his horse.

He was cautious in the livery barn. The place was silent and still, just right for an ambush, but he had no trouble and went back to the hotel. He ate a meal then left the hotel to look around the town. There was a light in the law office as he passed and he entered to find Frank Lambert eating his supper at the desk. The deputy put down his fork when Fenner entered.

'I was gonna come looking for you when I got through here,' he said. 'The men I sent out to trail your herd got back about ten minutes ago. They caught up with the rustlers, said they could hear the cattle bawling as the herd went through Pike's Pass, but they walked into an ambush when they tried to follow. One of them took a slug and the others came back for more help. I told them you'd be riding out tomorrow and two of them want to go with you. They are regular possemen and can be trusted.'

'Thanks. I could do with someone who knows the area. But I wouldn't ask them to take risks. I'll do my own fighting.'

'It's law business,' Lambert reminded him. 'We don't take kindly to rustling right on our doorstep, and some of your men were killed. I wanta hang someone for that.'

Fenner nodded. 'I'll be riding out on the trail of the herd at dawn. Tell your men to be at the livery barn and we'll ride together.'

He left the office and went along to a saloon. He was parched right through to the backbone, and tried to relax as he drank a couple of beers. A man approached him and Fenner stiffened, dropping his hand to his gun.

'I'm Tom Bisbee,' the man said. 'I rode with the posse that went out after your herd today. I guess you're Travis Fenner, huh?'

'That's me.' Fenner nodded. 'Lambert told me his men were back. You got shot up.'

'It wasn't too bad. One of the boys stopped a slug. You'll be riding tomorrow, huh?'

'Yeah. And I'll need someone to guide me.'

'I'd like to go with you. Jack Hilliard taking a slug made it personal for me.'

'Sure. Be glad to have you along. Just put me up close behind the rustlers. I'll take care of it from there. Have a drink.'

'Thanks.' Bisbee was an oldish man, at least forty, and seemed capable. He drank a beer with Fenner and then took his leave. 'It's been a hard day,' he said. 'I'll be at the stable before the sun shows.'

'I guess I'd better turn in.' Fenner stifled a yawn.

Bisbee departed and Fenner drained his glass, his gaze on the big room, taking in his surroundings from force of habit. He set down his glass and had turned towards the batwings when they were thrust open and two men entered the saloon. One of them was Silas Hegg. The lawyer was talking animatedly to a big, tough-looking man who was wearing twin guns on crossed cartridge belts, his face covered by the wide brim of his well-pulled-down hat. Hegg glanced around the saloon as he entered and his gaze fell upon Fenner, who was about ten feet from him.

'That's him!' Hegg yelled frantically and turned to flee. 'Kill him, Jake.'

Fenner set himself the instant he recognized Hegg, and his right hand was already gripping the butt of his holstered gun when Hegg's companion turned to him. Fenner saw at a glance that the man was Jake Quigley and surprise blanketed his mind, but his instincts were incorruptible. Quigley reached for his right-hand pistol in a surprisingly fast draw. Fenner set his own hand into motion. His gun came out of its holster, his thumb cocking the piece even before it cleared leather. He saw Quigley's gun lift but the big man was a split-second slower, and realization hit him as he tried to catch up.

The raucous blast of Fenner's pistol drowned all noise in the saloon. The walnut butt of the weapon kicked against the heel of his hand and smoke flared. Quigley rocked under the impact of the half-inch .45 slug which smacked dead centre into his enormous chest. His gun ceased its upward movement and his rising hand fell away as his ponderous strength lapsed. He absorbed the tremendous shock of the bullet. His mouth was agape under the effort of making an unexpected draw, his face twisted by shock and astonishment. He took a quick step backwards as his balance diminished, and then he sprawled sideways as death stole his control. He fell heavily, like a tree brought down in a storm, and crashed upon a small table, flattening it with his bulk. He rolled once and then was still.

Fenner cocked his gun and ran to the batwings while the occupants of the saloon were frozen by shock. He shouldered through the swing doors and paused on the sidewalk, gun lifted, its muzzle moving like the snout of a wild animal seeking its prey. He saw Hegg running away along the sidewalk, his short legs pumping as he tried desperately to gain distance.

'I got you covered, Hegg,' Fenner yelled, His voice seemed distant in his own ears, filled as they were with the shock of the shot that had killed Quigley. 'Hold it right there or you'll join Jake Quigley in hell!'

SIX

Hegg paused directly under the glare of a lantern and glanced back over his shoulder at Fenner. When he saw the uplifted gun in Fenner's hand his whole body slumped as he realized the futility of further flight. He raised his hands and stood motionless, afraid to move even a muscle in case he attracted a slug from Fenner's gun. Fenner strode along the sidewalk, his boots rapping the wood-work, spurs jingling. Hegg had barely made ten yards. His face was chalk-white in the yellow glare of the lantern suspended beside his right shoulder. Resignation showed in his fleshy face.

'You got some explaining to do,' Fenner rasped, jabbing the muzzle of his gun against Hegg's generous stomach. 'If you're carrying a gun then you better get rid of it pronto.'

'There's a .38 in a holster under my left armpit.' Hegg's voice was squeaky in fright. He looked as if his worst night-mare had materialized under his nose. His hands trem-bled, and he jerked as if Fenner had struck him when his pistol was taken from him. Fenner threw the weapon into the street.

Boots were pounding the sidewalk to the right and Fenner glanced over Hegg's head to see Bill Lambert coming to check on the disturbance. The deputy was breathing heavily when he arrived, gun in hand.

'What was the shooting about?' he demanded.

'Tell him, Hegg,' Fenner rasped.

The lawyer gulped and moistened his lips. He opened his mouth to speak but no sound emerged. He shook his head. Fenner jabbed him again with the muzzle of his gun.

'Spill it,' he rapped. 'Why did you tell Quigley to kill me when you saw me in the saloon?'

'Quigley?' Lambert was shocked. 'Do you mean one of the Quigleys of Q Bar over to Brushwood?'

'Yeah.' Fenner nodded. 'I met the three Quigleys yesterday on HF range. Moses offered to help me fight the rustlers but I got the feeling he was bluffing.' Fenner glanced at Lambert. 'Hegg took off from Brushwood after I rode out to HF to look around, and I got a hot reception from the crew Hegg put on the spread – had to kill most of them. Hegg knew his time had come because he cleared his money out of the bank and split the breeze. I sure didn't expect to see him in Twin Forks. I heard you had urgent business in Ellsworth, Hegg. So what's keeping you in this neck of the woods?'

'Did you tell Quigley to kill Fenner?' Lambert demanded.

Hegg remained silent, gazing disconsolately at the boardwalk. Fenner swallowed to clear his ears of gun thunder.

'Let's go back in the saloon,' he suggested. 'There are a dozen witnesses there.'

Lambert grasped Hegg by the arm and propelled him to the batwings. Men were gathering on the sidewalk outside the saloon, attracted by the shooting. Inside, the men present were recovering from their shock. Several stood around the body of Jake Quigley, just gazing down at the dead man. Lambert cursed softly when he saw the motionless figure, and shook his head.

'There's gonna be hell to pay over this,' he observed. 'I never thought I'd see the day a Quigley was gunned down. You beat him to the draw, huh?' Respect showed in the deputy's eyes. 'That makes you something special, Fenner, but you're gonna have to be better than that when Moses gets to hear about it.'

'The Quigleys can wait.' Fenner shrugged. 'You'd better start talking, Hegg. I wanta know what's been going on at HF. The crew at the ranch tried to kill me on sight, on your orders.'

Hegg shook his head. He moistened his lips. 'I don't know anything about that,' he said. 'I don't mix with people like the Quigleys.'

'Then what were you doing with Jake Quigley?' Fenner demanded. 'You told him to kill me the minute you laid eyes on me, and he reached for his gun without hesitation.'

'I wasn't with Quigley. I just happened to enter the saloon as he got there.'

'I heard you tell Quigley to kill me.' Fenner glanced around at the attentive townsmen. 'Did anyone see and hear what happened when Hegg and Quigley came into the saloon? I was on the point of leaving.'

Several of the men agreed with Fenner's account of the incident and Lambert made a note of them.

'That's good enough for me,' the deputy said. 'You're gonna see the inside of the jail, Hegg. Come along.' He grasped the lawyer's arm and led him from the saloon.

Fenner went with them and they walked to the law office, followed by a number of curious townsmen. When they were in the privacy of the office Lambert took a tougher line with Hegg, pushing the lawyer into a seat and standing over him.

'Come clean, you mealy-mouthed shyster,' he rasped. 'I've been getting reports of the trouble building up further north. Chris Arlen is keeping me informed. I know the Quigleys were banned from Brushwood, and they've got big reps as troublemakers. So what were you doing with Jake Quigley? And don't say you weren't in his company.'

Hegg shook his head. He seemed too shocked to be able to talk intelligibly. Fenner lost his patience.

'I got no time to wait for his lies,' he said. 'Throw him in a cell and leave him there until he can come up with a statement. I'm riding out in the morning, and maybe I'll get some of the answers I need from those rustlers. I saw Tom Bisbee in the saloon. He's gonna ride with me at first light.'

'Bisbee is a good man,' Lambert said. 'You won't find better than him. I hope you catch up with those thieves.'

'I'll get to them,' Fenner said confidently, and left the office.

He walked to the hotel, his thoughts deep and fast. Having to kill Jake Quigley was an unexpected twist in the sequence of events, and he tried to clear his mind of the inevitable outcome. He went to his hotel room to turn in, weary beyond belief, but found enough energy to clean his pistol before sleeping.

It was still dark when he awoke. He lit the lamp and sat up, impatient to hit the trail. Within minutes he was leaving the hotel. Grey dawn covered the town as his boots pounded the boardwalk, sending echoes across the street. He stepped down into the dust and went on silently, spotting a figure ahead as he neared the stable. He gave a low whistle and the man turned and waited for him to catch up. It was Tom Bisbee.

'I heard what happened when I left the saloon last night,' Bisbee said. 'You sure ain't playing games. But the Quigleys are top notch. Their kind are way above my head. I couldn't live with the likes of them. They're half human and half wolf.'

Fenner nodded, aware of what was coming. 'There ain't enough room on the range for them and me so they've got to go, because I mean to stay here.'

'I can't afford to get mixed up with them,' Bisbee said ruefully. 'I'm married, and I got a couple of kids. I'll ride with you far as Pike's Pass, but then I'll have to turn back.'

'Don't worry about it.' Fenner smiled. 'I can handle this alone. Those rustlers are signposting their trail. They'll be easy to catch up with. I rode with the Texas Rangers for five years and faced odds like this more than once. I won't lose much sweat over coming to grips with them.'

Bisbee was relieved, and turned around to return to his home. Fenner went on to the stable and entered to saddle up. He was impatient to hit the trail. His horse stamped and cavorted as he led it out to the water trough, and he gazed around at his surroundings while the animal drank its fill. The sun was peering over the horizon now, throwing light into the shadows, but there were no signs of the town coming to life. He swung into his saddle when the horse was through drinking and set off to the town grazing ground, where his chuck wagon was starkly outlined by the rising sun.

The cook's body had been removed in the night. Fenner dismounted at the wagon and found a gunny sack inside, which he filled with supplies and several boxes of cartridges for his pistol and rifle. He tied the sack behind his cantle and remounted to circle the ground where the cattle had grazed for two days, cutting across the trail they had followed up from the south and continuing to circle until he found the tracks made when the rustlers stole the herd. He reined in and looked around, his narrowed eyes picking out the direction taken by the thieves. Then he pushed his horse into a canter and set out for the reckoning. Apart from the trouble he had encountered around Brushwood, three of his men had been killed and his brother badly wounded. There was a big score to settle.

The herd had stampeded away from Twin Forks, heading west, but the rustlers proved they knew their job by gaining control quickly and turning the cattle into the north-west. Two thousand head of beeves left a trail a blind man might have followed, and Fenner pushed on, riding to the right of the trail to avoid any ambush that might be set, eating up the miles that separated him from his herd. The sun rose at his back and the heat increased until he was sweating.

Around the middle of the afternoon he spotted a cabin in the shade of a few oaks by a small stream. The little building was primitive, with a sod roof and a cow hide for the door. The trail left by his herd passed the back of the cabin and continued to the north-west. Fenner reined in beyond a ridge and studied the apparently deserted habitation. There was no stock around, no signs of life, and he rode out into the open and descended to the cabin, needing to check it out before continuing. As he passed a clump of brush just in front of the cabin a man arose from its cover and pointed a rifle at him.

'Who are you, feller?' The man's voice was filled with hostility. 'What do you want?'

Fenner reined in and sat motionless in the saddle, regarding the man, who was past middle-age, probably halfway through his fifties, dressed in dirty range clothes, with a greasy Stetson pulled low over his dark, unblinking eyes. There was suspicion and tension showing on his lined face, and his trigger finger was white-knuckled as he covered Fenner.

'I'm riding through,' Fenner replied. 'Reckoned to water my horse at the stream. I'm making for Brushwood.'

'You're too far west. You got to cut to your right over that ridge and keep going in that direction.' The man's narrowed eyes were regarding Fenner's outfit, and then he spotted the Big F brand on the rump of the horse. 'Say, that's the brand on the herd that went through here earlier. Are you riding with that bunch? They took my stock with them in passing. I reckon they would have killed me if I'd shown myself. Right salty bunch. The signs were, they had rustled those cows.'

'You're right about that. I'm Travis Fenner. I was bringing the herd up from Texas to stock the HF ranch north of here. The herd was being held at Twin Forks when rustlers hit it. Three of my men were killed.'

'And you're riding alone to get the cows back, huh?' The man shook his head. 'I counted eight men with that herd, mister. You got your work cut out, sure as my name is Rafe Spooner.'

'I reckon I can handle it.' Fenner noted that the muzzle of Spooner's rifle had dropped a little. 'Mind if I water my horse?'

'Go ahead. I'll ride with you to get my stock back, if it's all right by you.'

'No need for that. I'd hate for you to get killed by those thieves. I can handle the chore alone. I'll herd your stock back to you later, after I get the herd on HF. I'll have another crew by then. Did you get a look at the rustlers when they passed?'

'Yeah. Never saw anyone I knew. Saw a couple of horses I'd recognize again. Mebbe that's why you should change your mind about me coming along. I could mebbe point out some of that crew even if I saw them without the cattle. That would be a help if you don't catch up with the herd before it gets to where it's going.'

'Where's your horse?' Fenner queried.

Spooner chuckled. 'Well hidden. Water your bronc and go on. I'll come up with you before sundown.'

'Thanks.' Fenner smiled and touched the brim of his hat as he rode on to the stream. He dismounted and let his horse drink, pulling it away before it had taken its fill. Then he rode on, and shadows were creeping into the country by the time he spotted movement on his right. His gun seemed to leap into his hand to cover the figure that suddenly appeared, and he suspended the movement when he recognized Rafe Spooner, who emerged from cover and rode in beside him.

'You're right slick with that gun,' Spooner observed.

'You shouldn't have sprung your appearance on me like

an Indian,' Fenner countered. 'I guess I'm a mite nervous these days.'

'It's the only way to move around, trouble being what it is. That crooked bunch would have done for me if they'd caught me. I ducked out when I heard them coming. We can't be far behind the herd now. How'd you plan to get them beeves back?'

'Get ahead of them and shoot the rustlers as they come up. I'll nail the ones riding point and swing. The herd will run, but they'll be going in the right direction. Those riding drag will have to pass me to get to the cattle and I should nail a few of them.'

Spooner nodded. 'Sounds about right. We'll catch up about the middle of tomorrow.'

Fenner glanced at the sky as they rode on. Shadows were long upon the ground. Night was creeping in. He considered the travelling he had done since leaving Brushwood and estimated that HF was a day's ride to the north-east. He needed to get his boundaries fixed in his mind, and assumed that he was probably on home range right now.

'Have you been around here long?' he asked Spooner.

'Three years.' Spooner chuckled. 'That place of mine back there might not look much but its the start of the RS ranch. It takes time to build up a spread, and I'm in the throes of it at this time. Those rustlers wiped me out when they took my cattle. I'll be glad of the chance to hit back at them.'

They rode until it was too dark to follow the trail, and Fenner picked his campsite with care, aware that the rustlers might send a couple of men to check along their back trail for signs of pursuit. They put a ridge between them and the trail, ate cold food, then turned in. Dawn was close when they broke camp next morning, and they were on the trail before the sun appeared above the eastern horizon.

Around the middle of the morning, Spooner pointed ahead. 'I see dust,' he said. 'It won't be long now.'

Fenner had already spotted the dust that was rising from the slowly moving herd, estimating that they were some three miles to the rear. He studied the lie of the land ahead and turned east to bypass the herd. They slipped behind a ridge and pushed their horses into a faster pace. Thirty minutes later, Fenner halted and dismounted. He looked over the ridge and saw his herd strung out, moving under the constant urging of the rustlers. He counted eight riders, and a tremor of anticipation stabbed through him.

Spooner crawled up beside him and surveyed the scene, nodding at what he saw. They moved back off the skyline and prepared to go on.

'You want I should hang back near the drag and cut loose at them when you fire your first shot?' Spooner demanded.

Fenner nodded. 'You got plenty of shells?'

'I'm loaded for bear. I got enough for that crooked bunch. Looks like the herd will pass though a gully in that higher ground ahead. I reckon that would be the place to hit them.'

'You're right. Don't take any chances, Spooner.'

'No sweat,' the man replied with a grin.

Fenner went on, pushing his horse and keeping the ridge between himself and the herd. He met the rising ground and, estimating that he had passed the herd, dismounted to check his position, taking his rifle with him. He saw that the rustler riding point was entering the gully, followed by the bunching steers. Dust was rising thickly.

He hunkered down on the skyline and jacked a shell into the breech of his rifle. Sweat was running down his forehead and he cuffed back his Stetson and wiped it away. He felt no emotion when he drew a bead on the leading rustler's back. These thieves had killed three of his outfit. He fired, and the sharp crack of the long gun flung echoes across the gully. The rustler pitched out of his saddle, and had hardly hit the ground when the herd took off in panic, running blindly along the gully, hemmed in by the rocky walls and unable to turn back because of the following cattle.

Fenner reloaded and waited. He saw two riders down there amidst the fleeing herd, trapped by the crush of frightened animals, and they were lashing the cattle around them with their lariats to keep from being trampled. He fired at the nearest rider. The man toppled out of his saddle and fell beneath the wildly threshing hoofs of the fear-maddened steers. The sound of shooting from the drag of the herd came faintly to his ears as he fired at the third rider, wiping the man out of his saddle. He waited with cocked rifle, awaiting more targets. The pounding of the trampling hoofs sounded like thunder in the hills. Dust swirled.

Another rider appeared, trying desperately to keep his place in the herd, being swept along by the living tide of animals. Fenner lifted his rifle, but at that instant the man's horse lost its footing and rider and animal disappeared under the crushing hoofs. For long minutes Fenner watched his herd streaming through the constricted area of the gully, his teeth clenching when he saw a steer here and there falling and being swallowed up by the rush of terrified beeves. Then the tightly packed herd began to thin out, leaving in its wake a cloud of dust with just the odd straggler moving through it.

Fenner stood up and peered into the murk, looking for Spooner, and minutes after the last animal thundered by below the man appeared, jogging along the gully on his horse, his rifle held across his thighs. He spotted Fenner and waved, and Fenner replied by waving his rifle. Fenner hurried to his horse and mounted. His herd was no longer under the control of the rustlers. All he had to do now was stop the stampede.

He continued across the ridge and descended the other side. A cloud of dust partially obscured his cattle, but he was able to see that they had slowed and were beginning to graze. The animals were tired from their long haul up from Texas or they would have run for miles. He hit level range and rode towards the gully. Spooner appeared, waving his rifle, grinning widely because of their success.

'Knocking down the rustlers riding drag was like shooting fish in a barrel,' Spooner said. 'They never knew what hit them. Do we go back and check them out or go for the herd?'

'My only concern is for the cattle,' Fenner replied. 'The steers are so tired they should be easy to handle. I got a feeling we're on HF range now so I'll take the point and we'll keep 'em moving to the north-east.'

'I've ridden through here,' Spooner said. 'There's a line shack that belongs to HF about two miles ahead. Will one of your outfit be there?'

'If anyone is there he won't be one of my crew.' Fenner shook his head. 'Any idea whose range this is?'

'Q Bar.' Spooner spoke through his teeth. 'That's an outfit it ain't healthy to tangle with. We better get the herd moved on to HF before the Quigleys show up.'

'Jake Quigley won't come,' Fenner said. 'I killed him in Twin Forks last night.'

'The hell you say! Jeez! You're piling up a load of grief for yourself. Mind you, all the Quigleys need killing. They're range scum – bad all ways to the middle.'

'I'm wondering where the rustlers were taking the herd,' Fenner mused.

'Riders coming,' Spooner cut in, pointing to the right with the barrel of his rifle.

Fenner turned his head quickly and saw two figures coming from the direction he judged HF to lie. They came forward at a canter, moving wide around the herd to avoid alarming the animals.

'Looks like Harvey Crench and Bill Spencer, Circle C's foreman,' Spooner observed as the riders drew near.

'I met Crench in Brushwood. What kind of a man he is?'

'Honest, I figure.'

They sat their mounts awaiting the arrival of the two riders, and Crench seemed surprised when he recognized Fenner. He reined in and looked around at the herd, now grazing quietly.

'Howdy, Spooner? Good to see you again, Fenner. Where's the rest of your crew?'

Fenner explained, and Crench shook his head.

'That's the first setback those rustlers have had,' he opined, 'and you've only got to pass that line shack and you're on HF. We'll give you a hand to push the herd over there. I was at your headquarters and looked over those men you shot. Didn't recognize any of them. Someone's brought in a bunch of strangers to do their dirty work.'

'Hegg hired them.' Fenner spoke harshly.

'Talk in Brushwood is that Hegg lit out for safer range,' Crench said. 'I guess he got his fingers in too many pies, and mebbe burned them, too. He always came across as a shyster. I wouldn't have trusted him as far as I could throw a fully growed steer.'

'He didn't get far.' Fenner narrated his experience in Twin Forks, and Crench laughed when he heard of the shooting which ended Jake Quigley's life.

'That's good news,' he said. 'So you killed Jake. Someone should have done that a long time ago. Him and his brother Sarn should have been drowned at birth. You'll have to watch your back when Moses Quigley hears about it. Moses sets great store by his sons. He'll make a bee-line for you the minute he gets the news.'

'I got other things to worry about right now,' Fenner said. 'Let's get my stock on HF grass.'

They went for the herd. Spooner took up the drag and Fenner rode point while Crench and his foreman rode one either side of the herd. The animals were tired and moved slowly, but two hours later they had passed the line shack and the herd went on into a natural basin where a creek glittered in the sunlight.

'They won't stray far from here,' Fenner said, wiping sweat from his forehead. 'They'll need to rest up some and start putting on meat.'

'You'll need someone here to watch them in case rustlers turn up again,' Spooner said. 'I'll stay at your line shack until you can get another crew together. I can cut out my stock from the herd while I'm here.'

'Thanks.' Fenner nodded. 'I'll get another crew together soon as I can. Don't take any chances if trouble turns up. Just get the hell out of here and come to the ranch to alert me.'

Spooner grinned and rode towards the line shack.

Crench nodded as he looked around. 'We'd better get on back to home range,' he said. 'I reckon you'll do good now, Fenner. I'm ready to turn out if there's any more trouble. You only got to send me word.'

'Thanks, Crench. We're gonna have to fight this trouble, you know. It won't just go away.'

'You've made a good start.' Crench grinned. 'I'll send word to other local ranchers and we'll start making plans to tackle the trouble.'

'Thanks for your help. Before you go just point me in the direction of my ranch house.'

Crench obliged, and Fenner heaved a sigh as the rancher departed. He looked at his herd and considered the situation. There was much to do, and fast. He needed to hire another crew and wanted to check out the rustlers they had killed. He had to confront the men running the trouble in order to beat it. There were the surviving Quigleys to be faced, and he had to get back to Silas Hegg to discover what part the shifty lawyer played in the set-up.

He rode to the line shack to discover Spooner searching the place.

'There ain't much in the way of supplies,' Spooner said, 'but otherwise I can hold out until you get another crew.'

'I'll have Curly bring out some grub,' Fenner told him. 'Don't take any chances, huh?'

Spooner shook his head, and ducked when a bullet smacked into the doorpost beween them. They both dived into cover as the report of a rifle shot hammered and echoed across the illimitable range.

SEVEN

Fenner dived through the open doorway into the shack when a bullet struck the doorpost, and twisted and reared up, gun in hand, before Spooner could follow suit. He moved to the glassless window and peered out for gunsmoke. Spooner hunkered down in the doorway, Colt ready for action. The next instant a fusillade of shots hammered out the silence and slugs crackled and splintered into the shack. Fenner threw himself flat to the floor and kept low until the shooting faded, and when the tempo of the attack slowed he pushed himself up to return fire.

At least six attackers were outside. He caught a glimpse of flitting figures moving around and began to shoot at them, aiming each shot carefully, unmindful now of the lead that came back at him. He knocked down two figures and the shooting ceased abruptly. He held his fire in the absence of targets, listening to the dying echoes as he reloaded his empty cylinder.

'I hit one of them,' Spooner reported, 'but I don't see any of them now. Do you think they're pulling out?'

'I nailed two, and I reckon there were six of them when

they opened up.' Fenner peered through the window aperture, his eyes narrowed as he studied their surroundings. He could see nothing now, but caught the sound of receding hoofbeats. 'Sounds like they're pulling out,' he mused, standing up and lowering his gun to his side. 'Cover me while I take a look around outside.'

Spooner finished reloading his pistol and got to one knee just inside the doorway. Fenner stepped outside, ready to duck back into cover should the shooting restart, but nothing happened and he walked around the shack, moving out as he did so until he had made a complete circuit. He found a spot where someone had fired a number of shots at the shack – marked by several glinting cartridge cases – and looked around, mocked by the silence that had returned, although gun echoes seemed to be hanging on in the far distance. He went back to the shack, where Spooner was still crouching in cover.

'No one out there now,' he reported. 'Do you reckon they were more rustlers?'

Spooner shook his head. 'How many rustlers are there on this range? he queried. 'We've been knee-deep in them since yesterday.'

'And why did they pull out? They had us boxed in here.'

'We took out half of them soon as we started shooting.' Spooner grimaced. 'Mebbe they ain't got the stomach for fighting when they don't have the odds in their favour.'

'Maybe you're right. I think we'd better head out for the ranch. The sooner I get a crew together the better. You can't stay here. If they come back and catch you alone they'll kill you.'

Spooner did not protest and they left the shack and

caught up their horses. Fenner did not like the idea of leaving the herd undefended, but consoled himself with the knowledge that if it were stolen again he would be able to track it down. They rode out, and evening was drawing on as they cantered towards HF.

Night fell and they continued under the crescent moon that rose in the east. Spooner evidently knew where HF was located because he twice warned Fenner that he was riding too far north, and it was well past midnight when they spotted the collection of buildings that formed the Fenner ranch.

'I left Curly Brennan here,' Fenner said. 'He's an old fire-eater so we've got to be careful. He'll shoot first and ask questions afterwards. If we ride in openly he should hold his fire until we're close enough to call him.'

'You hope,' responded Spooner. 'I know that old coot well, and we better not take any chances with him.'

'Drop back and I'll go in alone until I'm close enough to sing out to him.'

Spooner reined in immediately. Fenner opened the gate and continued across the yard.

'Curly, are you awake?' he called.

'Sure am, and I got you covered.' Brennan's voice echoed across the yard. 'What are you doing back here, Boss? I didn't hear no herd coming in.'

'It's on HF grass now, down by the southern line shack,' Fenner replied. 'Is there any chance of getting some food at this time of the night? I got Rafe Spooner with me.'

'Come on in. I ain't seen Spooner in a coon's age. Is he riding the chuck line these days?'

Fenner called Spooner in and they rode to the cook shack, where Brennan had lit a lamp. The old cook was grinning as he raked up the damped-down fire and added fuel. He moved around the shack with the dexterity of long experience, preparing a meal. But his smile faded when Fenner acquainted him with the problems he had found at Twin Forks.

'Wish I could have been with you,' he growled. 'I don't get any fun these days. But one good thing happened while you were gone. Three of Henry's old crew rode in yesterday. They heard you were here and came looking for a riding job.'

'Where are they?' Fenner demanded eagerly. 'They can start right now.'

'I told them to come back in a couple of days, when I expected you back. Two of them rode on to Brushwood. Dick Langton is a top hand. I gave him a list of supplies I need from the store and he said he'd tote them in when he returns. I put in a big order for cartridges. Harvey Dent and Ed Parr are keen to be riding for you. Ed is in the bunk house, covering you from there, I hope. Harvey rode with Dick. I guess you can't do better than them three when the chips are down. They'll fight for the brand, Travis. They didn't want to quit when Henry was murdered but Hegg fired them.' Brennan went to the doorway of the shack and yelled into the night. 'Ed, are you awake?'

'Sure am, Curly. I got the cook shack covered. Everything all right?'

'It is now. The boss just rode in. Come on over.'

'It's a pity you didn't keep the three of them here,' Fenner observed. 'I could do with them riding herd. I reckon those rustlers will strike again before we're ready for them.'

'I know Langton and Dent by sight,' Spooner said. I'll

ride into town and fetch them after a bite to eat. I could be back here just after dawn.'

'They could go straight to the line shack from town.' Fenner mused. 'That would save time. Two of them just might be able to hold off the rustlers until I pick up another outfit.' He turned to the doorway as a tall figure stepped into it, a Winchester held in capable hands.

'Ed, this is Travis Fenner, Henry's nephew up from Texas. He's eager to get an outfit together soon as possible.'

'Howdy, Ed?' Fenner greeted, studying Parr and liking what he saw. The cowboy looked as if he knew one end of a cow from the other. 'I wish I had all of Henry's crew here right now. There's a lot of trouble facing the outfit at the moment, which will end in gunsmoke, but after that it will be straight cowpunching.'

'Best news I've heard since Hegg fired the crew,' Parr said. He was thin as a bean pole, with a long face, hollow cheeks, and dark eyes that glistened with an inner fire. 'I'm ready to fight for the brand.'

'Wait till you hear what Travis has done since he arrived,' Brennan said with a grin. 'You got a lot to live up to, Ed. You wanta a cup of java? It's the only time you'll get coffee off me in the middle of the night so make the most of it.'

Parr shook his head. 'I'll pass on that, Curly. Your coffee ain't no great shakes during the day so I reckon it can only get worse at night. I'll take a walk around the yard and keep an eye on things until you get through in here and put the light out.' He stepped back out of the doorway and faded into the shadows.

Fenner and Spooner ate the meal Brennan cooked for them and then Spooner set out for town. Fenner stood with Brennan and Parr in the silent yard. The night was still. The moon gave pale light to the ranch and countless stars studded the black mantle overhead. A breeze was blowing in from the west, carrying a multitude of scents and aromas from clear across the Rockies. Fenner struggled against the errant emotions that tugged at his mind. He was helpless in the grip of events, although he would never cease to fight those opposing him, whatever the odds.

'I guess there's nothing we can do now but turn in,' he said at length. 'It'll be dawn in a few hours. Why don't you two pound your ears for a spell? I'll stand guard for a couple of hours, then call you to take over.'

'I'm an old man and don't need much sleep,' Brennan replied. 'You need more sleep than me. You're the one gonna have to carry this fight through, Travis. I'll watch the place till the sun shows. Not much happens around here nowadays because there's nothing worth stealing since Henry died.'

'Except the spread itself. But I don't expect the thieves will tip their hand like that.' Fenner suppressed a sigh. 'I'll spread my blanket over by the corral and sleep with a gun in my hand.' He stifled a yawn. 'Just fire a shot if you need me for anything. These days, I sleep with one eye open.'

Parr went back to the bunkhouse and Brennan departed, toting his shotgun. Fenner unsaddled and turned his horse into a corral, then spread his bedroll close by. He sighed with relief as he stretched out on the hard ground, for the full extent of his weariness hit him hard the moment he tried to relax. He discovered that he could not sleep immediately. His mind was seething with problems, and thoughts of the uncertain future plagued him, but eventually he overcame the demands of the situation and stretched out into sleep. Blessed unawareness settled upon him and he lay unmoving until the sound of approaching hoofs alerted him and he arose with his pistol in his hand, cocked and ready for action, to find the sun was peering above the horizon.

Fenner looked around and saw two riders coming into the yard. Brennan was standing in the doorway of the cook shack, shotgun held ready, and Ed Parr was by the bunkhouse, toting a Winchester. The riders seemed to have peaceful intentions for they came at a canter across the yard to where Fenner was standing, his pistol down at his side. When they drew closer, Fenner recognized one of the men as Arlen, the deputy from Brushwood.

'Howdy, Fenner. When did you get in? I heard from Twin Forks that your herd had been run off and some of your crew murdered.'

Fenner narrated the events that had occurred, and Arlen shook his head in disbelief.

'That crooked bunch sure bit off more than they could chew when they figured to take over this range,' he observed. 'This is Dan Moore, Fenner. He's a deputy Sheriff Tooke sent over from Oak Ridge to help me through this trouble. I reckoned to leave him here to keep an eye on things until you got back, but you seem to be doing pretty well on your own. I sent word to Q Bar of Jake Quigley's death, but I didn't pass on any details. I reckon Moses will have ridden straight to Twin Forks, and by now he'll know that you killed Jake.'

'I wish you hadn't done that,' Fenner said in alarm. 'My brother is lying helpless in Doc Howard's house in Twin Forks. If Moses goes off half-cocked he might do some-

103

thing I'll rue for the rest of my life.'

'Frank Lambert is a good deputy,' Arlen said. 'I don't think you have anything to worry about.'

'I can't take that chance with my brother's life,' Fenner said bleakly. 'I've got to get back to Twin Forks soon as possible.'

'I don't reckon your horse will be up to it,' Arlen said. 'Dan, you're gonna be staked out here at least twenty-four hours so let Fenner use your horse.'

The deputy stripped his gear from the animal and Fenner saddled up with his own. He put a bridle on his own mount to take it along, intending to switch horses during the ride to maintain the fastest speed possible. He was swinging into the saddle of the deputy's horse when Brennan grasped the bridle.

'Why don't you let Ed ride with you, Travis?' the cook suggested. 'He's handy with a gun, and there's no telling what you might come up with on the trail. You need someone to back you.'

Fenner shook his head. 'It's my chore,' he said firmly. 'I can handle it.'

He touched spurs to the horse and the animal cavorted, incensed by the weight of a stranger in the saddle. Fenner brought it under control and departed. When he reached the open trail he set off at a mile-eating run, imagining his brother lying helpless in Twin Forks and Moses Quigley, thirsting for revenge, finding him there alone.

The miles slipped by as Fenner maintained a fast pace. He halted every thirty minutes to change mounts, and hammered over the undulating range. He bypassed Brushwood, gaining the trail south well beyond the town, and galloped on resolutely, hoping to reach his destination in time to protect his brother.

The sun had passed its peak when he finally sighted Twin Forks. Both horses were tired and he slowed the killing pace as he hit the main street. The town looked peaceful enough and he rode straight to the doctor's house, dismounting in a rush and leaving the horses with trailing reins. As he knocked at the door of the house it was opened by Mrs Howard, the doctor's wife, and one look at her expression was enough to warn Fenner that something was wrong.

'I'm so glad to see you, Mr Fenner,' the woman said. 'There's been some trouble in town. Moses and Sarn Quigley rode in just after dawn. They had heard about Jake getting killed. My husband is treating two men suffering gunshot wounds. One is Frank Lambert, the deputy sheriff, who had to shoot Sarn Quigley. Moses is in the saloon, drinking and shooting at anyone who goes near the place.'

'And my brother?' Fenner demanded.

'He's much better. The doctor was concerned that Moses would learn of his presence here and come to exact revenge.'

Fenner was filled with relief at the news. 'How bad is Lambert?' he asked.

'Barely alive. At the moment it's likely he won't survive. There was a shoot-out in the street. Moses knew you had killed Jake, and he's aware that your brother is here. He's using him as bait, knowing you will return.'

Fenner heard the crash of a shot from along the street and turned to face the direction from which it came. He saw small groups of men huddled along the sidewalks, staying under cover and watching the batwings of the saloon.

'Thank you, Mrs Howard,' he said, nodding. 'I'll go and have a word with Moses Quigley. It looks like he's scaring the whole town.'

He walked along the street to the first group of towns-men. Tension was showing on all faces.

'Is Moses Quigley in that saloon?' Fenner asked.

'He sure is,' one of them replied, 'and something's got to be done about him. He's stopped everything in town since he got here. Folks can't walk by the saloon without drawing a slug.'

'Is he alone?'

'He came in with Sarn Quigley. But Lambert shot Sarn. There's been hell to pay.'

'I've heard about it.' Fenner walked on, easing his pistol in its holster. When he reached the nearest corner of the saloon he flattened against the wall and eased forward to peer through a window. A gun crashed inside the saloon and glass flew as a bullet shattered the window Fenner was using, but he had ducked away the instant he saw Moses Quigley at the bar lifting his gun.

'Quigley. This is Travis Fenner,' he called. 'I hear you're waiting for me so come on out and face me.'

Quigley's gun crashed again and more glass flew.

'If you don't come out I'll come in and get you,' Fenner called.

'Come ahead. I've been waiting for you.' Quigley's voice was hoarse. 'You killed my boy Jake.'

Fenner entered an alley and made his way to the rear of the saloon, ducking down below a window when he passed it. He drew his gun as he tried the back door of the saloon, and slipped into the building when the door opened. He heard another shot fired in the bar room and cat-footed along a corridor to an open doorway giving access to the bar. He entered, passing under the flight of stairs that led to the upper rooms.

Moses Quigley was standing with his back to the bar, a pistol upraised in his big right hand. He was watching the batwings and the front windows, his left elbow on the bar.

Fenner moved out from under the stairs. 'You wanted to see me, Quigley,' he called. 'Here I am.'

Quigley moved fast for a big man. He came swinging round, his gun cocking as he faced Fenner. His craggy face was contorted, his eyes showing the wildness of a maddened steer. He thrust his gun forward, and Fenner shot him in the chest. Dust puffed from the dirty fabric of the big man's shirt. Quigley rocked back on his heels under the impact but did not go down. He returned fire, and Fenner ducked, the slug crackling by his left ear.

Fenner triggered his gun, aiming for the centre of Quigley's broad chest, and saw dust spurt again from the man's shirt. Quigley lumbered backwards an uncertain step. Blood was spreading across his shirt front. He sagged but did not go down. His gun muzzle faltered and he used his left hand to bolster the weapon. Fenner fired again. His shot struck Quigley's gun and tore it from the man's grasp. The heavy weapon thudded on the boards.

Quigley swayed like a tree being uprooted in a storm. His eyes were closed. He lifted his hands away from his body, attempting to maintain his balance. Then he fell forward on to his face, his impact with the floor shaking the saloon to its foundations.

Fenner heaved a long sigh as he went forward to look at the Q Bar rancher. Quigley was dead. Fenner's first bullet would have killed an ordinary man. He looked up as the batwings were thrust open, and saw Doc Howard entering.

'You can't do anything for him, Doc,' Fenner said. 'He's work for the undertaker.'

'Sarn Quigley is dead,' Howard said heavily. 'I couldn't save him.'

'How is Lambert?'

'He might pull through. It's strange, but I thought Quigley would live and Lambert might die.'

'That's the way it goes.' Fenner sighed. 'And my brother? How's he doing?'

'He's coming along nicely. He's got a good chance now the Quigleys are dead. Moses came to my house. He'd heard about your brother, but he didn't want to kill him. He was using him as bait – said you'd be forced to come back to protect him.'

'And he was right.' Fenner nodded. 'Have you seen my trail boss today?'

'Bill Blick. Yes, this morning. He's not as well as he makes out. He couldn't get out of bed although he tried hard. You better go see him. He'll have heard the shooting.'

Fenner nodded and left the saloon. He walked along the sidewalk to the hotel, pushing through the crowding townsmen, ignoring their excited questions, and went up to Blick's room. The wounded trail boss was sitting up in bed holding a loaded pistol. His relief was evident when Fenner walked in on him.

'I've been worried sick,' Blick said. 'I'm as good as tied to this bed and there's all that action going on. I heard the Quigleys were in town. What was the shooting about?'

Fenner told him and Blick shook his head.

108

'I wasn't able to go to Albie when I heard the news,' he said sadly. 'They could have killed Albie for all the use I was.'

'You were shot trying to protect our herd,' Fenner said. 'You've earned a rest. Anyway, I got the herd back and it's eating HF grass right now.'

'Tell me about it. How'd you manage it? Those rustlers knew what they were doing, and there was about eight of them.'

Fenner explained and Blick relaxed.

'I'm going back to HF now,' Fenner said. 'It's tough there right now. But I need to talk to Silas Hegg before riding out. He might be ready now to do some talking. I want you to stay around here when you can get on your feet, Bill. Your job is to take care of Albie. You got that?'

'Sure thing. I should be able to get up tomorrow. I'll make better progress when I'm on my feet.'

'I'll see you later.' Fenner walked to the door, then paused. 'You got any dough on you?'

'Enough for what I'll need. Don't worry about me, Travis. I'll bring Albie to HF soon as he's able to travel. You take it easy, huh?'

'I'll do what I have to,' Fenner responded, and departed.

He went along to the law office to find an oldish man there, sitting at the desk reading a weeks-old newspaper.

'I'm Travis Fenner. Who are you?'

'Hank Whitlock, the night jailer. They got me in because Lambert was shot. You brought the herd from Texas, huh? The one that was stolen the other night. Lost most of your outfit, too. You're getting all the bad breaks, mister. What's happening now along the street? I heard that Moses Quigley is holed up in the saloon, waiting for you to show.'

'You don't have to worry about Moses any more,' Fenner said. 'All the Quigleys are dead now. You've got Silas Hegg, the lawyer from Brushwood, in a cell, huh?'

'Yeah. He's been telling me it's illegal to keep him behind bars because he ain't done nothing wrong and there are no charges against him. Me, I just do like I'm told, and the word is to keep Hegg behind bars until he's been investigated.'

'I'm heading back to Brushwood shortly and I'd like to talk to Hegg before I leave.'

'Sure thing. It was you put Hegg behind bars, wasn't it? Never did trust shysters. They allus have to try using the law for their own ends. There's been some bad trouble over in Brushwood, by all accounts, and Hegg must be mixed up in it.' Whitlock got to his feet and took a bunch of keys from a nail in a doorpost. He unlocked the door and stepped aside. 'Hegg's the only prisoner I got. If you took him out of here I could go home.'

Fenner entered the cell block and looked around. He saw Silas Hegg seated on a bunk in the cell nearest the door. The lawyer was staring moodily at a blank wall, his face showing the depths of despair. He did not move even when Fenner called his name.

'Hey, Hegg,' Fenner called, grasping the barred door and shaking it. 'Stir yourself.'

Hegg looked up. His expression changed when he recognized Fenner and he sprang up and came to the door, grasping the bars until his knuckles showed white.

'You've got to get me out of here,' he said desperately. 'I heard shooting a while back. Was it Moses Quigley?

110

He'll come for me when he hears I was with Jake when you killed him.'

'Moses has threatened to kill me, and I shot his son in self-defence. What he'll want to do to you for pushing Jake into a fight with me doesn't bear thinking about.' Fenner spoke harshly, hoping to bluff Hegg into an admission.

'I'll do a deal with you,' Hegg said desperately. He seemed totally unnerved. 'I didn't have anything to do with the crookedness going on around Brushwood. I was coerced into it by those men who would stop at nothing to get what they want. They threatened to kill me if I didn't go along with them.'

'You don't have to take the blame for anything you didn't do,' Fenner encouraged. 'Just tell me the names of the guilty men and I'll see to it that they get the blame for their actions. I got a number of questions that puzzle me, and if you can answer them to my satisfaction I might be tempted to turn you loose, after I have checked that you've come up with the truth.'

'Can I trust you?' Hegg's voice tremored. 'I have to get out of here. I'll be killed when those in Brushwood get wind of what's happened in Twin Forks, and I'm not the man you want. I guess you're keen to know who killed Henry Fenner, huh? I can tell you that, and everything else, but only when I'm free.'

'You're not in a position to bargain,' Fenner told him. 'Give me the facts and I'll check them out. If I find you've told me the truth I'll come back and turn you loose. That's the best deal you can get. Take it or leave it. I'm gonna get to the bottom of what's been going on, with or without your help, so you better take advantage of my offer because there's nothing left for you. I'm in a hurry and

I'm heading back to Brushwood to finish what I've started.

'Take me with you,' Hegg pleaded, 'and I'll spill the beans about the others. Don't leave me here. Quigley will come for me, and I could tell you everything you need to know.'

Before Fenner could make up his mind about Hegg the silence of the town was shattered by a terrific blast of gunfire. Hegg turned and threw himself face-down on the bunk in the cell and Fenner turned and ran back into the office, drawing his gun as he did so.

EIGHT

Hank Whitlock was standing at the window in the law office, peering out at the street, when Fenner entered from the cells. Shots were being fired outside, and Fenner heard voices shouting. He crossed to the jailer's side and looked out at the street.

'What's going on?' he demanded.

'Six men rode into town. I looked out when I heard their horses. They stopped outside here, drew their guns and fired into the air. Now they're riding along the street, shooting at windows.'

'You got any idea who they are?' Fenner saw some of the riders firing their pistols into the air.

'Nope. But they're calling for Moses Quigley. Do you reckon they're some of Quigley's outfit?'

'I wouldn't know.' Fenner went to the door and opened it. He moved into the doorway and looked along the street. Four riders had reached the saloon. Two of them dismounted and entered the building, one of them reappearing immediately, shouting excitedly that they had found Moses Quigley. The rest of the riders rode to the saloon, dismounted, and went inside.

113

Fenner could see townsmen peering out at the street from cover, and no one was making any effort to discover the reason for the disturbance. He waited, watching to get the reaction of the newcomers to the death of Moses Quigley. Two of them emerged from the saloon and walked to the nearest building. One hammered on a door and, when there was no reply, kicked it in. They both went into the building to emerge shortly dragging a townsman between them. They took their prisoner into the saloon.

'It doesn't look good,' Whitlock observed. 'I wish Frank Lambert was here.'

A shot blasted inside the saloon and a moment later the man who had been dragged in was thrust out and dumped apparently lifeless in the street. Fenner turned cold inside, and drew his pistol to check the weapon. He reloaded spent chambers in the cylinder and reholstered the weapon.

'I'll take a look along the street,' he said. 'I might be able to learn something.'

'It ain't your job to do law work,' Whitlock protested.

'There's no one else around to do it, and if those riders are Quigley's outfit then they are my business.'

He left the office and went along the sidewalk to step into the nearest alley, where he paused to look around. The men in the saloon were not keeping watch, and Fenner moved forward again to duck into the next alley, working his way closer to the saloon. He was about to go on when two of the men emerged from the saloon, swung into their saddles and came back along the street at a canter. Fenner drew his gun.

He showed himself in the alley mouth when the riders drew level, covering them with his pistol. Both men made

114

as if to draw their guns but refrained at the last moment.

'In here,' Fenner rasped. 'Keep your hands away from your guns.'

The men obeyed, riding into the alley under the menace of Fenner's ready muzzle.

'One at a time, lift your guns and drop them in the dust,' Fenner ordered, and when they had complied he said: 'Now step down off those broncs and get your hands up.' He waited until they had done so. 'Tell me who you are,' he rapped.

'We ride for Q Bar,' one of them replied. 'Moses Quigley is dead in the saloon.'

'I know.' Fenner nodded. 'I killed him, and I'll tell you something you don't know. Sarn Quigley is dead. Where were you two going?'

'To the law office. Lou Jagger wants to talk to the deputy. There's gonna be hell to pay over Quigley's death.'

'Jagger?' Fenner frowned. 'He's the two-gun man who hangs out in Tipple's saloon in Brushwood, ain't he?'

'The same, and he's hopping mad.'

'Is Jagger leading your bunch?'

'Sure is. He was Quigley's man in Brushwood. Came out to the ranch with word that Fenner was riding back here, but Moses had already left for Twin Forks so Jagger brought us along to back him up. You wanta come along and talk to Jagger?'

'I'll get around to seeing him when I'm ready,' Fenner replied. 'What happened to the townsman who was dragged into the saloon?'

'He wouldn't tell Jagger what he wanted to know so he was killed. That's what you can expect from Jagger.'

'You were going to the law office, huh? So drop your

115

hands and start walking. I'll put you in jail and then attend to Jagger. Don't try to warn your pards or I'll back-shoot both of you. Now move, and do it steady.'

The two hard cases could not but obey with the muzzle of Fenner's gun covering them. They left the alley and walked towards the law office, their boots rapping the boardwalk. Fenner remained more than an arm's length behind them, a cold sensation nestling between his shoulder blades. They reached the office without incident and entered. Whitlock was waiting inside for them, the cell keys in his hand.

'That took a lot of cold nerve,' Whitlock observed.

'It's not over yet,' Fenner replied. 'Search these two and we'll put them behind bars. That bunch is led by Lou Jagger. They ride for Q Bar.'

'It was Tom Billings they dragged into the saloon and then tossed out.' Whitlock said. He searched each of the prisoners in turn, placing the contents of their pockets on the desk. 'It was cold-blooded murder.'

'They said Jagger shot him dead.' Fenner's tone was unemotional. 'So we know what to expect. Let's put them away and I'll see what I can do about the rest of them.'

'You can't go up against Lou Jagger alone,' Whitlock protested. 'He's like greased lightning with his pistols.'

'If Jagger was alone I'd take the risk,' Fenner said. 'Are there any men in town who would turn out for the law?'

Whitlock shook his head. 'There's half a dozen men who turn out for posse-work when needed, but I don't think they'd step into this. Lou Jagger is too well known.'

'That's what I thought.' Fenner addressed the prisoners as Whitlock unlocked the door leading into the cells. 'You got anything to say before we put you away?'

Neither man spoke and they were locked in a cell. Fenner led the way back into the office. He paused before a gun rack and inspected the long guns chained in it.

'I'll take that Greener twelve-gauge.' He pointed to a double-barrelled shotgun glinting with a bluish sheen.

'You ain't thinking of facing that bunch in the saloon, are you?' Whitlock frowned as he produced a key and unlocked the gun rack. He passed the Greener to Fenner, who inspected the weapon.

'I need to get back to Brushwood soon as I can, and I'm not about to ride out leaving those hard cases loose,' Fenner said. 'Give me some shells for this gun.'

Whitlock produced a box of shotgun cartridges, shaking his head while Fenner loaded the weapon. Fenner put four extra shells into a breast pocket. He went to the street door but paused in the act of departing.

'Will you come and back me up?' he asked Whitlock.

The jailer heaved a long sigh. His face was pale, and Fenner thought he would refuse, but he nodded reluctantly and took another shotgun from the rack.

'It ain't right that you should try it alone,' he said, loading the twin-barrelled weapon and putting spare shells into his pocket. 'It's against my better judgement, but let's get it done.'

'Take some handcuffs along,' Fenner said. 'We'll take prisoners if we get the chance.'

Whitlock grinned although he was highly nervous, and produced several sets of handcuffs. Fenner took two pairs and tucked them in his gunbelt.

They left the office. When they reached the nearest alley, Fenner turned into it, making for the back lots. He was sweating in the heat but his nerve was ice-cold.

Whitlock kept a couple of paces behind him. They reached the rear of the saloon and Fenner drew a deep breath as he paused to remove his spurs. The back door opened to his touch and he cocked the shotgun as he entered, followed closely by Whitlock. Loud voices sounded in the big bar room as they moved towards it.

'Where in hell have Pete and Rafe got to?' someone demanded as Fenner entered the bar.

Fenner paused when he could see four men at the bar. He recognized Jagger immediately – the only one dressed in a store suit. The four were standing in a tight group. All were drinking. Fenner motioned Whitlock off to his left, then levelled the shotgun and stepped forward.

'Throw up your hands,' he rasped.

The quartet at the bar froze their actions, although their heads turned quickly to look at Fenner and Whitlock. Jagger was in the act of drinking and paused with the glass to his lips, his dark eyes glinting as Fenner moved forward. Whitlock kept pace with him, and moved around to the left to cover the four men from a different angle. The shotguns were a menace that could not be ignored, and daunted the hard cases at close quarters. Silence settled over the big room.

'Get your hands above your shoulders,' Fenner rapped, pausing at the corner of the bar. 'Turn your backs to me, spread out to a yard between you, then stand very still.'

The men obeyed reluctantly. Jagger was on the right of the line.

'You're Travis Fenner,' Jagger observed. 'I saw you in Brushwood. It was you killed Moses, huh?'

'Right first time.' Fenner was tight-lipped. 'Now shut your mouth. You on the left, throw down your gun. If you try to get smart you'll get a barrel of buckshot all to your-self.'

The man lowered his right hand, took his gun butt between finger and thumb and lifted the weapon from his holster. It thudded on the floor.

'Now lie face-down on the floor and keep your hands away from your body,' Fenner said coldly.

The man obeyed, and Fenner repeated the process until all four were disarmed and stretched out on the floor. He glanced at the silent Whitlock, who was grim-faced but steady, the twin barrels of his gun covering the four men.

'Get them cuffed while I cover them,' Fenner said. 'They ain't likely to give us trouble now.'

Whitlock obeyed, his fingers trembling as he snapped cuffs around the men's wrists. Fenner tucked the butt of the shotgun under his left armpit and drew his pistol with his right hand.

'You can get up now,' he said crisply, and the four men scrambled to their feet. Jagger was scowling but remained silent. Fenner handed his shotgun to Whitlock and searched the prisoners. He found a .41 hideout gun under Jagger's jacket, nestling in the armpit.

'You're making a big mistake,' Jagger said.

'The Quigleys made the mistake of trying to grab HF range,' Fenner replied. 'Who murdered my uncle?'

'Is he dead?' Jagger demanded, and grinned.

Fenner lashed out with his pistol, slamming the long barrel against Jagger's skull. The gunman dropped to his hands and knees, his hat falling off as he shook his head. Fenner hit him again, crashing the gun against Jagger's right temple. The gunman groaned, collapsed and lay still.

'You three pick up Jagger and head for the jail,' Fenner ordered.

The prisoners obeyed without comment and they left the saloon and started along the sidewalk. A number of townsmen emerged from cover and came to surround them.

'I guess you can handle this now,' Fenner said to Whitlock. 'I need to be getting back to Brushwood. Have you sent word to the sheriff that Lambert is out of action?'

'Not yet.' Whitlock shook his head. 'I'll have enough help now to handle these prisoners. I'll keep them locked in the cells until I hear from Sheriff Tooke. I'll send a man to Oak Ridge, and there'll be another deputy on his way here by tomorrow.'

'Someone murdered Billings.' Fenner gazed at the motionless figure lying in the dust in front of the saloon. 'One of those two men we got in jail said Jagger did it. Don't take any chances with these hard cases. You don't need them running loose again. I'll drop by the jail when I'm ready to ride out and pick up Silas Hegg. I plan to take him back to Brushwood.'

Whitlock nodded and Fenner holstered his pistol as the townsmen escorted the prisoners to the jail. He looked along the street and saw Doc Howard standing in the doorway of his house. He walked along the sidewalk towards the doctor, feeling suddenly ill at ease. His fingers trembled as he looked at them and he clenched his hands. There was a hollow sensation in the pit of his stomach and he realized that he was long overdue for some food. He needed to get back to HF, but would have to take time out for his personal needs or he would never make it. He had been pushing himself too hard.

'The town owes you a big vote of thanks,' Doc Howard said when Fenner reached him. 'I went down to the saloon when Tom Billings was shot. He was murdered in cold blood.'

'I saw it.' Fenner nodded. 'They said Jagger did it. I need to be riding back to Brushwood but I've got to take time out to eat, and these horses need food and water.'

'I'll take care of them while you eat,' Howard said. 'You'll find them in the livery barn when you're ready to ride. There's a restaurant down there on the left.'

'Thanks, Doc.' Fenner went on along the sidewalk. The fire had gone out of him. He was having trouble keeping his spine rigid. Unsteadiness assailed him and he almost tottered as he paused at the door of the restaurant, but made an effort to shrug off the bad feeling. He entered the eating house, sinking down into a seat at a corner table and leaning his elbows upon it to keep himself upright.

A waitress approached and took his order. Fenner sat motionless, fighting a sensation that robbed him of strength and filled him with nausea. When the food arrived he had to force himself to eat, and it was not until he had lined his stomach with the meal that he began to feel any improvement. By the time he followed the meal with two cups of strong coffee he was almost back to normal.

He went back to the doctor's house and Mrs Howard took him to see his brother. Albie was asleep, his face pallid, sweat beading his brow. His chest was heavily bandaged. He did not seem to be breathing, but the pulse in his wrist was beating strongly when Fenner checked it.

'He's going to be all right, barring complications,' Mrs Howard said. 'He regained consciousness around dawn this morning. Right now he's sleeping normally.'

'I have to be leaving shortly.' Fenner spoke harshly. 'There's some business in Brushwood that won't wait. I'll be back soon as I can make it.'

He departed, taking with him a picture of his brother's pale face, and once again his determination was flowing strongly. He went to the stable and prepared the two horses for travel, then rode along the street to the jail. A crowd of men was standing outside the law office and they parted quickly, respectfully, to let him through when he stepped down from his saddle.

Whitlock had Hegg ready and waiting for him when he walked into the office. Hegg was pale and grim-faced. Fenner grinned at the man's apparent discomfiture.

'I guess your plans have taken a big knock, huh?' Fenner demanded.

Hegg shook his head silently.

'Come on then. I'm taking you back to Brushwood. Arlen will be pleased to see you, no doubt.'

Fenner escorted Hegg out of the jail and they mounted the horses. Fenner sighed heavily as they left town. The open trail lay before them, and he set a steady pace, his mind working over the situation. What had he accomplished? He was certain that the men he had killed were responsible for stealing his cattle and killing his men. The Quigleys had showed their hand and he'd had no compunction fighting them. He looked at Hegg, riding silently a couple of yards ahead, and touched spurs to his mount to draw level with the lawyer.

'How did you come to be in Jake Quigley's company when you walked into the saloon back in Twin Forks?' he demanded.

'I told you.' Hegg was thin-lipped and desperate. 'I happened to walk into the saloon as he was entering.'

'That won't wash so you better change your story. Try telling the truth. I'm not a law man. If you give me the lowdown on what's been going on around Brushwood I might be inclined to turn you loose. Who wanted my uncle dead? Was it your idea to steal HF? I think there's more to what happened than I've turned up, so if you want a deal then I'm listening.'

Hegg moistened his lips but did not speak. Fenner studied the lawyer's profile, noting the stern set of his face.

'It's all right by me,' he added when Hegg remained silent. 'Keep your mouth shut if that's the way you feel. Just remember that men have been murdered in this business, and you're a prime suspect. You'll stretch rope if I hand you over to Arlen in Brushwood, and you don't act like a man who doesn't care about his life. Think about it. We've got a long way to go, but you better decide one way or the other before we hit town. The law will want an accounting from you, and if they don't find anyone else who had a hand in the crookedness then they'll throw the book at you. Murder is a hanging offence, so I'll expect to see them take you out one fine morning, put a rope around your neck and swing you into hell.'

He dropped back a couple of yards and rode steadily, pleased with the way events had shaped. Miles slipped by beneath the hoofs of their mounts. Hegg sweated profusely, and repeatedly mopped his face with a big handkerchief. He became more and more nervous the nearer they got to Brushwood, but it was not until the town showed in the distance that he reined up and faced Fenner.

Night was falling. The sun was fast disappearing beyond the western horizon and shadows were long upon the ground. Fenner noted Hegg's agitation and was elated.

'Well?' he demanded.

'Will you turn me loose if I tell you what you want to know?' Hegg demanded.

'I'd have to check out anything you told me.' Fenner shrugged. 'I don't know that I need your confession. I've done all right so far, and when I ride into Brushwood I expect the rest of the plot to come to light.'

'It won't do that.' Hegg shook his head emphatically. 'There's too much beneath the surface. How can I trust you? I could tell you what's been going on and you could still turn me over to the law.'

'That's the chance you'll have to take. Let's start at the beginning. Who shot my uncle, and why was he killed?'

Hegg looked at him intently, trying to assess his chances of going free. The daylight was almost gone now, and the breeze had cooled considerably. Fenner was sweating, and parched through to the backbone.

'Kane Tipple spoke to me one day.' Hegg spoke hesitantly, weighing his words. 'He wanted to go into the ranching business. He owns most of the businesses in town, and didn't want to spend a fortune financing a cattle spread. He was planning to take over HF because it is the biggest ranch in the county. He'd heard that Henry Fenner had no kin, and wondered what would happen to the place if Henry died suddenly. I explained about you down in Texas. I knew about you because Henry had me write up his will a few years ago. Tipple said you could be dealt with when you arrived to take over HF on the death of your uncle. I figured that Henry had at least another ten years to live, and was shocked when I heard a few days later that he had been murdered.'

'Did you tell the law about Tipple's intention to take HF?' Fenner demanded.

'I saw Tipple and accused him of having Henry killed. He admitted it freely. He'd paid Lou Jagger to commit the murder, and threatened me if I didn't toe the line. I had to get you up from Texas so Jagger could kill you. Jagger knew the Quigleys down in Texas. They were all rustlers together, and the first part of their plan was to run off all HF stock. Moses Quigley was keen to go along with the plan, and his bunch soon handled the rustling. The rest of it you know. Arlen paid Bud Snark to confront you when you arrived.'

'Arlen?' Fenner frowned. 'Is the deputy sheriff in this?'

'I'm telling you he is.' Hegg's face was almost invisible in the growing darkness. 'You ain't got much hope of beating this thing, Fenner!'

'Don't tell me about my chances,' Fenner retorted. He turned his head swiftly and glanced over his shoulder. A sound had attracted him from behind. He slipped his right foot out of the stirrup even as he turned, and was diving out of the saddle when the shadows were split by a tongue of flaring muzzle flame. He heard the crackle of a slug passing his head. The crash of the shot blasted and echoes rolled. Amidst the tumult, Fenner heard a thin cry of anguish from Silas Hegg.

Fenner landed on his left shoulder and rolled to the left. His horse had run in the same direction. He twisted around, gun in hand, and heard a thud as Hegg fell out of his saddle. The lawyer hit the ground almost on top of him. Echoes faded. Fenner lay gazing into the shadows,

his eyes dazzled by the gun flame. He heard someone calling orders to other men, and a cold chill stabbed through
him when he recognized Lou Jagger's harsh voice.

NINE

Fenner reached out his left hand and his fingers encountered Hegg's motionless figure. He pressed his hand against the lawyer's chest, discovering that Hegg was dead. Jagger was urging his men to close in, his raucous voice filled with triumph. Fenner moistened his dry lips, wondering how the gunman had managed to escape from Twin Forks. He cocked his gun and prepared to fight, his mind vibrant with determination. Jagger had murdered his uncle.

A gun crashed and a slug screamed over Fenner's head. He fired at the flash and rolled to his right as two more guns flamed. Bullets smacked into the hard ground near him and he fired twice in quick succession, aiming for gun flashes. Then there was a pause and silence followed the dying echoes of the shooting.

Fenner reloaded his spent chambers, plucking shells from his cartridge belt, his eyes narrowed to pierce the gloom as his fingers did their work. He closed the gun and snapped a shot at a faintly moving shadow to his left, flattening out before return fire could reach him. He slid to his left, keeping low, blinking rapidly against the brilliance that dazzled him.

Jagger was silent now. Fenner estimated four men against him and fancied they would try to surround him. He eased back in the direction his horse had taken when the shooting started. There were no sounds now. The breeze blew into his eyes, making them water, and he rolled easily, putting distance between himself and Hegg's motionless body.

He heard a horse grazing, tearing at bunch grass with strong teeth, and got up into a crouch and moved quickly. Shots crashed instantly and he flung himself headlong, but the bullets did not come near him. He moved again, saw the horse and crawled forward until he could grasp its trailing reins. He sprang into the saddle, spurred the animal, and sent it galloping away into the night. Shots blared but he was untouched.

Fenner heaved a sigh as he rode towards Brushwood, and now his thoughts were concentrating on Hegg's admission. If the lawyer could be believed then Kane Tipple was the man he needed to confront. Then he thought of Arlen, the deputy, and reined up to sit thinking about the situation while he watched his surroundings, ears strained for sound. If the local law was crooked then he had to stay out of town. He took his bearings from the lights of Brushwood and circled to bypass it. When he hit the trail that led to HF he sent the horse forward as fast as he dared in the uncertain night.

An hour before midnight he reached the yard of HF and dismounted at the gate. The ranch headquarters was in darkness but he expected someone would be on guard. He called out and Curly Brennan's voice came from the dense shadows surrounding the cook shack.

'Come on in, Travis,' the cook yelled. 'It's been too damn quiet around here since you rode out.'

Fenner walked his horse across the yard and found Brennan standing in the doorway of the cook shack, a shotgun tucked under his right arm. Fenner took care of his horse while he told Brennan of his experiences, and the cook was loud in his appreciation of the shocking news.

'I'm sure glad those bullying coyotes the Quigleys are dead,' Brennan observed. 'Perhaps now the rustling will stop. I kept Ed Parr with me. He's in the bunkhouse. He'll stand guard the last part of the night. Langton and Dent came back from town with Rafe Spooner, and I sent the three of them to the south line-shack to keep an eye on the herd you brought up from Texas. Spooner reckons to ride with you for a spell, until you can get an outfit together.'

'Rustle me up some grub and coffee and I'll tell you the rest of my news,' Fenner said.

'Sure thing. Come on into the shack.'

Fenner lounged against a wall and watched Brennan preparing a meal. He gave the cook details of Hegg's death, and the revelations the lawyer had made to gain his freedom.

'I'm not surprised Tipple is involved in this,' Brennan ventured in a harsh tone. 'But Arlen seemed to be a decent sort as a lawman. It's a pity you didn't kill Lou Jagger when you had the chance. He's a tough one all right, and you're gonna have to kill him before this is over, you know.'

Fenner nodded. He sat down to eat the food Brennan

had prepared. Tiredness was pulling at him and he found it difficult to keep his eyes open. He ate quickly, as if afraid he might not get time to finish the meal.

'I'm gonna light outa here soon as I've finished,' he mused. 'It won't take Jagger long to figure that I've decided to give the town a miss, and he'll be coming here for a showdown. I need to face him because he shot Uncle Henry in the back, but I don't want to tangle with him until I think the time is right. I want to get the drop on Tipple first. I don't know what to do about Arlen. If he's crooked then he'll have to be faced, that's for sure.'

'I've got an idea you might not cotton to,' Brennan said. 'Ride over to Oak Ridge and talk to Sheriff Tooke. He's a tough old lawman, honest as the day is long, and he'll take a big load off your shoulders.'

Fenner shook his head. 'Nope. I got to do this my way. I'll ride into Brushwood just before dawn and get the drop on Tipple.' He paused, considering. 'Where's the deputy who came in here with Arlen before I rode to Twin Forks?'

'Dan Moore, you mean. He left just after you did. Borrowed Parr's horse, saying he had to get back to town fast.'

'Is that how Jagger knew Moses Quigley had gone to Twin Forks?' Fenner mused. 'Jagger turned up there with some gunnies just after I arrived and played hell until I threw him in jail. But he got loose somehow, and caught up with me just outside Brushwood.'

'The bad men seem to have friends everywhere,' Brennan observed. 'You got to watch your step, Travis. Put one foot wrong and you'll be dead.'

'It's been like that ever since I hit this range,' Fenner

observed. He finished eating and drank the coffee Brennan had made, then arose from the table. 'I'm heading for Brushwood now. That's where I'll find the men responsible for this trouble, and I've got to face them to put an end to it.'

'I don't like the thought of you heading to town alone. Go to the line shack and pick up the men there. They'll back you all the way. I told them they'd likely get mixed up in shooting and they said it goes with the job. You need someone to side you, Travis. The minute you show your face in town the gunnies will be out to get you. Jagger will have passed the word by now. Those men controlling the business will know the Quigleys are dead so they won't give you a chance.'

'I'll think about it.' Fenner stifled a yawn and shook his head impatiently, 'Heck, I'm gonna have to turn in for a couple of hours,' he decided. 'I ain't fit to fight in this state. I'll hit the sack back of the corral. Call me around four, huh?'

'Yeah. Now you're talking sense. You look plumb tuckered out, and you've got nothing to hurry over. That trouble sure ain't going away. It'll still be there tomorrow, waiting for you to shoot it full of holes. By the way, there's something I forgot to tell you. A gal rode in here this afternoon. Real pretty, she was, and asking for you. Said her name was Ruth Sheldon and you told her to head out here if she got any kind of trouble. She wouldn't say what the trouble was, and took off soon as I told her you'd gone to Twin Forks.'

'Ruth was here!' Fenner shook his head. 'I sure hope she didn't get any trouble on my account. But she wouldn't have come for any other reason. Something must have

131

happened in town to scare her. Why didn't you keep her here. Curly?'

'I ain't the kind of man who would be stupid enough to try and keep a gal against her will.' Brennan shook his head. 'No sir! I told her to come back tomorrow some time. I figured you'd be back by then.'

Fenner suppressed a sigh and went out to the corral. He picked up his bedroll and moved away around the pole fence before shaking out his blanket. He dropped down wearily, placed his pistol close to hand, and was asleep in a matter of minutes. When he opened his eyes again it was to find the sun climbing up over the horizon, and he sprang up, cursing Brennan.

'Why didn't you call me like I asked?' he demanded, peering in at the doorway of the cook shack.

Brennan was cooking breakfast. He looked up and grinned. 'I didn't have the heart to call you,' he replied. 'You was sleeping peaceful as a babe, and you sure needed to rest up. That trouble will be waiting for you so don't worry about it. Have some breakfast before you pull out. You'll get a different slant on things now the sun is up. What you've got to do is whittle down the odds against you so they don't get too big to handle.'

'If you fight a snake you shoot off its head and the rest of it dies,' Fenner observed bleakly. 'That means I go straight for the top man, and if I get him the rest will drop out of it.' The smell of bacon cooking on the stove filled the cook shack and made him aware that he had not eaten properly in several days. 'I'll head for town and face up to the man Hegg said is running the business.'

Brennan nodded, aware that he could do nothing more to persuade Fenner to be careful. Ed Parr came in for breakfast carrying a rifle, which he leaned against the back of his chair when he sat down. Fenner was impatient to be on the move, but forced himself to eat a meal. He was relieved when it was over, and went out to saddle his horse.

The rapid tattoo of an approaching rider alerted Fenner as he tightened his cinch and he looked towards the gate to see Rafe Spooner coming across the yard, pushing his mount hard. Fenner stifled a pang of shock, aware that more trouble must have struck during the time he had been asleep. He had been certain that he should be in Brushwood just before dawn, but had missed his chance. He should have been out attacking his enemies instead of resting up. Time enough to rest when the trouble was over.

Spooner slid out of his saddle when the horse skidded to a halt beside the corral. Fenner saw a patch of blood high on the right shoulder of the man's shirt and hurried to him. Spooner leaned against the corral gate, hanging his head for a moment, his shoulders heaving. His face was pale, his eyes filled with shock and pain.

'Rustlers hit the line shack during the night,' he gasped. 'They ran off the herd, and some of them kept us pinned down until they got the herd clear. They fired the shack and we had to bust out. I was hit but Dent got me away. When the gunnies pulled out I headed here for help while Dent and Langton trailed the herd.'

'Any idea who the rustlers are?' Fenner slid an arm around Spooner to support him as he staggered.

'We couldn't tell in the dark. There were about a dozen of them. They pushed the herd north.'

Brennan came out of the cook shack carrying a medical box. He examined Spooner and then set to work to doctor the wound.

'It ain't too bad,' Brennan said at length. 'Don't look to be any bones broken, Rafe. I'll patch you up before we send you into town to see the doctor.'

'I'm riding after the herd,' Fenner said. He fetched his horse and swung into the saddle. 'Keep your eyes open for trouble around here, Curly.'

He touched spurs to his mount and, when he was clear of the ranch, rode at a fast clip for the line shack. The sun baked him as it moved across the sky, but he was unaware of his natural surroundings as he pushed on. It was early afternoon when he sighted the ruined line shack, and moved in cautiously. The place was little more than a burned-out wreck, and he stepped down from his saddle to look around closely. The herd was gone, as he had expected, and he moved on foot in a wide circle around the shack, checking for tracks. He found a lot of sign indicating that the rustlers had headed north-west.

Swinging back into his saddle, he prepared to take out after the herd, but caught a glimpse of movement in the brush. His gun seemed to leap into his hand and he covered the four men who emerged from cover and came towards him, on edge until he recognized Harvey Crench leading the riders. He holstered his gun as the Circle C rancher lifted a hand.

'I heard there was shooting over this way,' Crench said when he arrived. 'I don't see your herd around. Has it been rustled again?'

Fenner recounted what had happened and Crench shook his head. The men with him were looking around, hands close to their holstered guns.

'If you're riding after the rustlers then me and my boys will go along,' Crench said. 'I sent word to a couple of my neighbours and expect them to follow when they've gathered their outfits. We've got to tackle those rustlers, and this looks like the right time to start.'

'I've got a couple of men trailing the herd,' Fenner said. 'Let's follow tracks.'

They rode fast in the direction taken by the herd. Fenner and Crench rode ahead, intent on the trail. Fenner scanned their surroundings from time to time, looking for signs of Dent and Langton and watching for trouble. Two hours of riding took them into broken range, and Crench reined in.

'We're close to Q Bar now,' he said. 'With the Quigleys dead the rustlers might be using that place as their headquarters.'

'We'll know more about it when we catch up with the rustlers,' Fenner replied. 'Let's keep moving. I need to see the herd before sundown.'

They went on. The sun moved over to the last quarter of the western sky and shadows began to lengthen. The herd had entered a gully, and rising ground on either side formed natural fences, but the herd was still moving north. Fenner suddenly noticed that the tracks they were following had ended and he reined up to dismount and look around, wondering at the efforts the rustlers were making to remain undetected.

'The rustlers have blotted out the tracks of the herd,' he observed.

'Unless them cows sprouted wings and flew to new pastures,' Crench replied.

Fenner walked around the gully. It was only twenty feet wide here, and rocky, but his experienced gaze noted the attempts that had been made to wipe out the tracks. He saw the prints of a couple of horses and assumed that they had been made by Dent and Langton following the herd. Leading his horse, he walked up the gully, and covered many yards before the tracks resumed. They continued, and after another mile the gully widened into a valley, where Fenner saw his herd bunched in the middle distance.

'There's a couple of men moving around that beef,' Crench observed. 'I don't see anyone else here.'

'They could be Langton and Dent,' Fenner said. 'Let's go talk to them.'

The two riders spotted them but did not run.

'They're Dent and Langton,' Crench said as they galloped forward. 'Hegg fired them from HF after your uncle was killed.'

Fenner had not met the two cowboys, who sat their mounts stolidly, hands on the butts of their holstered guns until they recognized Crench. Then they relaxed and waited for the party to reach them.

'Howdy, Mr Crench?' One of them spoke with a trace of suspicion in his voice. 'I'm sure surprised to see you riding in here. This herd was stolen off HF during the night. We followed it here and found it unattended. There's sign the rustlers rode off to the west, and Quigley's place is over that way. We're waiting for our new boss to show up. Rafe Spooner stopped a slug in the shooting at the line shack and rode to HF to get help.'

'This here is your new boss, boys,' Crench said, jerking a thumb at Fenner.

'Glad to know you, Boss. I'm Dent. This is Langton. Curly Brennan took us on. I hope we did the right thing by following the rustlers.'

'You sure did.' Fenner nodded. 'Curly told me about you, and I'm glad you showed up when you did.' Fenner liked the look of the two men. Dent was short and sturdy, every inch a cowhand, and had a round face with honest eyes. Langton was tall and thin, dark, and his brown eyes were filled with a harsh glitter.

'I'm sure sorry your uncle was killed, Boss,' Langton said tensely. 'Me and Dent looked around some after it happened, and we'd have taken on the killer if we'd got a line on him. But we had no luck, and then Hegg fired us.'

'I'll tell you all about it when I've got the time,' Fenner said. 'But Hegg is dead now, and I know for a fact that Lou Jagger killed my uncle. I'll be taking it up with him when we've handled these rustlers. Moses Quigley and his two sons are dead.'

The softly spoken words shocked both cowboys into silence. Crench shook his head in disbelief.

'Heck, you've wiped out about half the men I suspected of handling the rustling,' the Circle C rancher said.

'That's what I figure,' Fenner replied, 'and I'm riding into Brushwood when I can get around to it to confront the rest. It's time to put an end to the crookedness that was hatched out against HF.'

'We'll ride with you,' Crench said firmly. 'All the ranchers around here have lost stock to the rustlers. Now we've started we better go on with it or it'll never end.'

Fenner nodded. 'Let's track down the rustlers and put them out of business. We'll play the cards as they fall.'

Dent and Langton rode to where they had seen tracks left by the rustlers, and Fenner got down from his saddle and looked around. He dropped to one knee and inspected hoof prints closely, then nodded and returned to his horse. They moved off at a fast clip, following the tracks of some half-dozen horses.

Thirty minutes later Crench broke the tense silence that enveloped them. 'It looks like we're riding straight into Q Bar,' he observed. 'The ranch is just over that ridge ahead. We better not ride in there until we find out what's waiting for us. I always figured the Quigleys were behind the rustling, and it's a real shame they're not here to answer for their actions.'

They reined in below the ridge and Fenner and Crench crawled up to the skyline. The Quigley ranch was nestling in a low valley, looking deserted in the late evening sunlight, but there were a number of horses in the corral by the bunkhouse and a column of smoke was rising from the chimney of the cook shack.

'How do we handle this?' Crench asked.

'I reckon to sneak in there, take a look around, and listen to some talk before I decide how to handle it,' Fenner said.

'I'd better go with you. You won't know faces like I do.'

'It could be real dangerous down there,' Fenner observed. 'If there's trouble and we get separated we could start shooting at each other. I reckon you should stay up here with the rest while I find out what's going on.'

Crench laughed harshly. 'In for a dime, in for a dollar, huh?' he said. 'I guess you better wait for full dark before moving in. I ain't about to argue with you. You seem to have done pretty good on your own.'

They went back to the others and waited out the last minutes of the dying day. Fenner sat and cleaned his pistol, his mind filled with conjecture. He had not had a moment's peace since his arrival in the county and tiredness was blunting his natural alertness, but he knew there could be no rest until the bad men were put down. Full dark settled and he got to his feet, charged with determination. Crench and the others accompanied him to the top of the ridge and hunkered down there while he descended to the valley to walk the hundred yards or so to Q Bar headquarters.

The night was now full dark but Fenner had little difficulty finding his way. There were lights showing in the various buildings before him and, drawing nearer, he could hear a guitar twanging in the bunkhouse. He made for the fence skirting the yard and slipped between the poles, keeping to the shadows as he made his way to the side of the house, curious to see who was in occupation with the Quigleys dead.

He walked around the house, finding only one window brightly lit, and that was in the big room overlooking the porch. Fenner paused at the front corner of the building and looked along the porch to check it was deserted. There were three saddle horses standing at a hitch rail in front of the porch. He went back to a side window and peered into the room. Shock stabbed through him. Lou Jagger was sitting at a desk, his arms folded, listening to two men standing before the desk who were talking at great length. Fenner could just hear what was being said. The two men were giving Jagger a report about the rustled herd. He stayed close to the window, watching closely. Jagger's face was set in harsh lines, showing displeasure, and the gunman shook his head several times as he listened.

Fenner glanced around the room. He saw a woman seated in a big chair in the far corner. He frowned, for she seemed familiar. She was looking away from him, showing little more than her profile, and seemed to be sitting awkwardly. It was then he noticed that she was tied hand and foot, cruelly roped to the chair in over-tight bonds. His shock increased when she glanced towards the desk where Jagger was seated, for he recognized her as Ruth Sheldon, the waitress from the eating house in Brushwood.

What was she doing here after turning up at HF the previous afternoon? Fenner's brows pulled into a frown as he considered. Had the trouble she feared caught up with her? She said something to Jagger in a high-pitched voice that was laced with fear. Fenner did not hear what she said, but Jagger's voice was loud enough to carry to him as he snapped at Ruth, his tone filled with displeasure.

'Tell me what I wanta know,' Jagger snarled. 'You were followed from town yesterday and you rode into HF. So what were you doing there? I heard you'd got friendly with Fenner, and that's enough to get you killed. Tell me what's going on and I'll turn you loose, but if you keep your mouth shut then you'll get what your brother got.'

'You killed Mike!' Ruth yelled, struggling against the rope binding her.

'I've killed a lot of men.' Jagger's evil-expressioned face took on a smug smile. 'And I'll kill a lot more before this is finished. I want to get my hands on Travis Fenner. He's come up from Texas and played hell with our plans. In a matter of days he's killed the Quigleys, Bud Snark, Deke Purdy and God knows how many of our crew. He scared the hell outa Silas Hegg, who took off like a yellow rabbit, and when Fenner caught up with Hegg in Twin Forks that shyster spilled his guts about our set-up. I had to kill Hegg myself to put a stop to the rot Fenner started. Now I want Fenner before things get even worse.'

'What makes you think I know where he is?' Ruth demanded. 'I don't know, as it happens, and I wouldn't tell you even if I did. If you had any sense, Jagger, you'd get out of it before Fenner does catch up with you. I saw in the very first minute I set eyes on him that he is one of those men who can't be killed by polecats like you. Oh, you'll keep trying to do the impossible, but then he'll catch up with you and it'll be your turn to die. He's like an avenging angel sent down to rid us of your kind. The writing is on the wall, Jagger, but you can't see it.'

Jagger sprang to his feet and crossed the room, cursing as he towered over the helpless girl, his right hand upraised to strike. Fenner flinched as the big man slapped Ruth across the face, rocking her in her seat, but her defiant smile did not slip, even when a trickle of blood dribbled from a corner of her mouth.

'I'll see you down in the dust before this is finished,' she said, her smile widening. 'You'll pay for what you've done and I'll dance on your grave when they bury you.'

Jagger wheeled away from the girl in disgust and turned on the two hard cases standing silently in front of the desk.

'Larter, take her outa here and kill her. Bury her in that draw back of the house. I ain't got the inclination to waste more time on her. Go get it done now.'

'I ain't in the business of killing women, Lou,' Larter protested. 'I've done just about everything you ever asked me since we came up from Texas but I draw the line at beefing a female. Turn her loose, why don't you? She ain't gonna cause you any trouble.'

'Jeez, no wonder this business is going wrong.' Jagger

141

paused in the middle of the room and lifted his right-hand gun from its holster. 'I'll kill her myself if you're so finicky. Is it too much to ask you to bury her?'

'I ain't doing the killing,' Larter said firmly. 'Anything else is fine by me.'

Fenner caught his breath as Jagger turned back to the helpless girl. He suddenly realized that his gun was in his hand, cocked and ready for action, and knew he could not stand by idly while Ruth was murdered in cold blood.

TEN

Jagger lifted his pistol and eared back the hammer, grinning as he waggled the gun in front of the girl. Ruth's face was ashen, her eyes wide in fright. Fenner could see Jagger's intention to shoot. When the gunman began to level the six gun, he waited no longer. He thrust forward his gun, crashing the muzzle hard against the window and shattering the glass. Jagger swung around and turned his gun to meet Fenner's threat. Fenner fired two quick shots that thundered as one and his slugs smashed into Jagger's chest. Jagger fell backwards, his gun blasting, and the man called Larter jerked and jackknifed to the floor. His companion turned to the window, instinctively reaching for his gun, and Fenner shot him. Gunsmoke plumed across the room.

Fenner transferred his gun to his left hand and smashed out the remaining shards of window glass before reaching in and unfastening the catch. He opened the window, climbed over the sill and checked Jagger in passing, although he knew the gunman was dead. When he went to where Ruth was seated she was gazing at him as if he were a ghost. Gun echoes were fading slowly, and

Fenner yawned to rid his ears of the shock of the rapid detonations.

'I don't know how you came to be in such a bad place,' he said, holstering his gun and attacking the knotted rope binding her, 'but we've got to get you out of here before any of Jagger's sidekicks show up.'

'Where did you come from?' Ruth gasped. 'I went to HF yesterday to warn you. I heard in town that you were going to be arrested for murdering Mack Tomlin. Arlen was gathering a posse together to come out and pick you up.'

'I'm expecting trouble from Arlen,' Fenner mused. 'So he's gonna use the law to get rid of me.'

'Arlen is crooked. He's in with Tipple.' She clutched at his arm as he pulled the rope from her. 'How can you hope to beat this crooked set-up if the law is against you?'

'Let's get out of here before someone comes to check on the shooting.' Fenner drew her towards the window. He heard boots thumping on the porch outside and ran to the window, dragging Ruth with him. He bundled her out through the aperture and heard her yelp as she sprawled on the hard ground outside.

The door of the room was thrust open and a man appeared, gun in hand. Fenner drew his gun and he and the man fired together. Fenner went down on one knee as he fired and felt the shock of a bullet passing through the high crown of his Stetson. The man staggered and twisted, then fell to the floor. Fenner turned and dived through the open window. He tucked in his head, rolled over, and landed on his shoulder blades on the ground outside, gaining his feet in one swift movement.

A gun thundered inside the room and bullets came

spraying through the darkness. Fenner ducked, wondering about the girl. He angled his gun upwards, fired at the dark figure that appeared at the window and a man came tumbling out into the shadows.

'Over here,' Ruth called urgently, and Fenner moved swiftly towards the sound of her voice. They collided in the dense shadows, and Fenner grasped her as she fell away from him.

'Let's get out of here.' He held her arm, not wanting to lose her in the darkness, and led her away from the house. Behind them the night was filled with gun thunder and whining slugs slashed through the close darkness. Fenner angled away, and they gained the cover of a stand of oaks, beyond which he could hear the gurgling of running water.

He paused under the trees and looked back, listening intently for sounds of pursuit. He reloaded his pistol, snatching shells from the loops of his cartridge belt. Voices were shouting in the dense shadows surrounding the house, although Fenner could see nothing. Then he heard the sound of hoofs rattling the hard ground and recalled the horses standing at the porch. The riders were coming towards the trees as if they knew which direction he had taken, and Fenner's lips pulled back into a silent snarl of defiance as he turned to Ruth, invisible beside him. He grasped her arm to find out exactly where she was, and leaned towards her to talk in an undertone.

'Stay here and don't make a sound,' he said hoarsely. 'I'll come back for you. Get behind a tree and stay close to it. I'll call out to you when I return so don't move until you hear my voice.'

She did not reply. Fenner moved out, worried by his

sense of responsibility for her. He walked towards the sound of the approaching horses, figuring that they would not expect him to stand and fight. He cocked his gun and peered around, ready to continue trading lead.

He had noticed, when he checked the porch at the house, that one of the horses was grey, its light colour glinting in the lamplight issuing from the front window. Now he saw a faint outline of it moving towards him, and caught a glimpse of the rider, outlined against the starry sky. Another rider loomed up just behind the grey. Fenner raised his gun and triggered it fast. Reddish flame spouted from his muzzle and the weapon bucked against the heel of his hand. Gun echoes marred the peacefulness of the night.

The rider of the grey uttered a thin cry that cut through the raucous crash of gunfire. He vanished from the saddle as if wiped out by a giant hand. Fenner squinted and swung his gun, loosing a shot at the second rider. He saw the man fall sideways, and then the grey was upon him. He sidestepped the animal to avoid being run down, turned in the direction it was moving, and reached out with his left hand as he dived forward to grab it. His fingers caught hold of trailing reins as he holstered his gun and reached for the saddlehorn with his right hand. He leapt at the horse, hurling himself up into the saddle.

The grey stopped instantly and Fenner almost pitched over its neck. He regained his balance and looked around but was unable to see anything. His eyes were dazzled by the flashes that had erupted. He heard nothing and hoped it would stay that way. Turning, he rode slowly towards the stream, guided by the sound of running water. When he was closer he called the girl's name urgently, and relief filled him when she replied in a low tone, guiding him with the sound of her voice. He dismounted and trailed the reins, telling himself that when he had got her clear he could come back and handle the rest of those killers.

'I've got a horse for you.' His voice was pitched just above a whisper. He was looking back even as he spoke, ears strained for sounds of pusuit. But now nothing moved out there. The ranch was silent and still. 'How did you come to be taken prisoner?' he asked, his voice echoing under the trees.

'Larter, one of the men you killed in that room, confronted me when I left your place yesterday. He'd followed me from Brushwood on Jagger's orders. Jagger spoke to me twice in town after that evening you tangled with Snark. He was concerned that I might know something of his plans and pass it on to you. Larter said I had no business going to HF so he brought me here and kept me prisoner. Jagger didn't turn up until later today, and you know the rest. He was going to kill me. I knew he was evil. He shot my brother so Snark would get the job as town marshal.'

'Jagger's dead now.' Fenner spoke with a trace of satisfaction in his voice. 'Let's get moving. Climb into that saddle. You can go back to HF. When you reach it stay there until I show up. There's gonna be more shooting before this is done, or I miss my guess, and I can't wait to get at it. But I want you safe. Can you find your way in the dark?'

'I know this range,' she replied. 'What are you going to do?'

'I've got six men with me, and we'll do what is necessary. They're waiting back of a ridge. Mount up now and get out of here. You'd better make a detour if you can or you might get picked up again by the wrong men. Jagger doesn't miss many chances, it seems. Don't forget to sing out when you reach HF. Curly Brennan will be watching, and these are dangerous times.'

He held the horse while she mounted, then handed the reins to her and stepped back.

'Thank you for showing up when you did,' she said softly. 'Jagger was going to kill me. You saved my life. Good luck.'

She turned the horse and rode away. Fenner listened to the receding hoofbeats, while watching his surroundings. Nothing stirred, and when full silence returned he went through the trees and made his way back to where he had left Crench and the others. As he began to ascend the ridge a voice challenged him from the shadows. He gave his name and Crench emerged from cover.

'We got a mite worried when we heard the shooting,' Crench said. 'What happened?'

Fenner explained and Crench laughed hoarsely.

'It was a bad day for the rustlers when you arrived in Brushwood,' he said. 'What do you reckon we should do now?'

'I was thinking of going back to Q Bar and finishing the job I started.' Fenner peered off into the night, listening intently. Hearing nothing, he continued: 'Upon reflection that doesn't seem like a good idea. With Jagger dead I don't think those rustlers will do anything on their own. They might even pull out, thinking the game is over. I reckon we should go to Brushwood. If we can get the drop on Arlen and Tipple I reckon it'll be all over, unless some more of their kind crawl out of the woodwork.'

'That sounds about right,' Crench said. 'All but the bit about tangling with Arlen. He's the law, whatever he might be doing on the side, but let's get to it. The sooner we end it the better.'

'I'll handle Arlen,' Fenner vowed, wishing now that he had not sent Ruth off on her own, but he had feared that her presence would have been an embarrassment. He wanted her to be clear of danger, and it was in the forefront of his mind that if he made a mistake in his judgement then anyone riding with him could die as a result, and he did not want anyone's death on his conscience.

They crossed the ridge and were challenged. Dent arose when he was satisfied they were not rustlers. Then Langton and Crench's three men appeared, all carrying rifles.

'What about your herd?' Crench demanded. 'You can't ride off and leave it this close to the rustlers. That's asking for trouble. Do you want us to stay with the beeves till morning then bring them back to HF?'

Fenner knew by the tone in Crench's voice that the rancher did not want to tangle with Arlen, and he took the easy way out.

'Thanks for the offer,' he replied, 'I prefer to ride alone when there's shooting to be done so stick with the herd. Let it come back at its own pace tomorrow, huh?'

He saddled his horse, checked his gun, and rode out. A weight seemed to lift from his mind as he headed for HF. He felt deeply obligated to the girl and needed to check that she had reached the ranch safely before riding on to Brushwood about his own business. He descended the gully and continued across the darkened range, relying on his sense of direction to travel unerringly through the night. It was close to dawn when he spotted a small square of yellow light shining in the distance and closed on it steadily, slowing to a walk as he rode nearer.

He dismounted way out of earshot to conceal his approach, and tethered the horse in lush grass by a stream. He stood for a time, listening intently, testing the atmosphere like a coyote. Night noises surrounded him but he heard nothing unnatural, yet the light in a window of the ranch house bothered him for he knew Curly Brennan preferred to be in the dark through the long hours of the night. He began to approach the house from one side.

Ruth had been a side issue, yet he had not hesitated to step in and save her because she had come out from town to help him, placing herself in peril. He appreciated the risks she had taken. He hoped she was safe inside the house. By the end of another day the trouble here should be at an end. All he needed to do was face Arlen for an accounting and then confront Kane Tipple, and anyone else who cared to step forward and try to put him down. The grim activities of the past days had narrowed the play down to two men.

His thoughts meandered as he slid between the poles of the fence surrounding the house. He paused to check his gun, looking around and listening intently as he did so. A keen breeze was blowing into his face. The silence of the night was complete. Then a horse in the corral stamped and whickered. Fenner's lips pulled tight when his horse down by the stream replied, the sound travelling easily through the greying darkness. He heard a porch board creak. The sound caused him to freeze, his gun coming to hand as he peered towards the dark pile of the house with its single rectangle of yellow light warning that all might not be well.

He waited, and heard the sharp sound of a door being opened, then closed. Someone had been standing on the porch and must have heard the whinny of his horse coming from a spot where no horse should be at night. He did not think Curly would move around in the dark, but Ed Parr might. He crouched and eased towards the house, ready for action.

He had to look through that lighted window. It would be dangerous because he would reveal his presence if there was a guard about. But it had to be done. He angled off to the right, making for the nearest front corner of the house, moving one step at a time, looking around and straining his ears for sound. He gained the corner and stepped on to the porch. A board creaked loudly. Flattening against the wall, he leaned forward and looked through the window. Shock hit him when he saw Ruth seated in a chair. Curly Brennan was lying on the floor. Ed Parr stood in a corner, his wrists shackled with a pair of handcuffs.

There were two other men in the room. Both were wearing law stars on their chests and holding drawn guns, although there was no one to threaten them except Ruth. So a posse had arrived at the ranch, Fenner thought, but where was Arlen? The deputy had to be around.

At that moment a board creaked to his left and Fenner whirled towards the sound, his gun hand lifting with the speed of a spiking snake. He saw a shapeless figure on the porch, in the act of rising from a chair, and orange flame spurted towards him from the shadows. A slug struck his hat like a flash of lightning, catching the left side of his head just above the ear. He staggered, feeling as if a mountain had fallen on him, and crumpled on the dusty boards of the porch as the raucous crash of the shot blasted through the silence. Then everything blanked out in a cascade of flashing stars. . . .

Fenner came back to consciousness slowly, flitting in and out of dim awareness like a swinging batwing door. It was like trying to awaken from a nightmare. He was unable to open his eyes and look around normally. In the background he could hear an unintelligible drone of voices that irritated him because he could not understand what was being said. He tried to will himself back to full consciousness but the effort needed was too great to produce. Glaring light began to hurt his eyes and he blinked, trying to force his eyelids open, but they seemed heavy, like slabs of rock, and he subsided again, until he heard Ruth's voice clearly.

'Is he dead?' she demanded. 'Have you killed him? What kind of a lawman are you, coming in here and setting an ambush like a criminal?'

There was such bitterness in her tone that Fenner felt obliged to spare her more uncertainty. He opened his eyes and a figure swirled before him for some agonizing moments before it settled into Arlen, who was holding a pistol and looking pleased with himself.

'He ain't dead,' Arlen said, 'although he should be. I shot him from a couple of yards and only grazed his skull. Must have a head like a rock.'

'Untie me and let me look at him,' Ruth insisted. 'What kind of a lawman are you? I always thought you were a decent man.'

'I'm doing my job,' Arlen replied. 'Fenner is wanted for murdering Silas Hegg. I wasn't about to take any chances with him. He's been on the rampage ever since he hit this range. Nobody was safe. He never asked questions, just shot to kill anyone who got in his way. You told me yourself that he was at Q Bar earlier and killed Jagger and several other men.'

'Jagger was a killer, and those other men were rustlers.' Ruth's voice tremored. 'Jagger was getting set to kill me when Fenner shot it out with him. He rescued me, got me away, and sent me here, thinking I'd be safe. I've told you all this but you won't believe me. What have you got against Fenner?'

'He broke the law.' A dogged note crept into Arlen's voice. 'He over-stepped the mark and he ain't gonna to get away with it.'

'Who told you he shot Hegg?' Ruth persisted. 'You're relying on the word of a killer.'

'I can't talk about my sources of information.' Arlen laughed. 'Fenner will get his chance to say what happened, but I got witnesses who saw it all.'

Fenner tried to stir but felt as if his head was nailed to the floor. He made an effort to concentrate and his eyelids flickered open. When he looked around the room it seemed to tilt and swing and he closed his eyes again hastily.

'He's coming to,' one of the possemen reported as Fenner managed to move his head at last. He lifted it slightly and looked around. His vision was blurred. He dropped his head back to the floor with a dull thud. Pain stabbed through his skull and he stifled a groan.

'You're a hard man to kill, Fenner,' Arlen observed.

'Get up if you can. Don't give me any trouble or I'll take you back to town face-down across a saddle.'

Fenner pushed himself into a sitting position and supported himself with his hands on the floor and his arms braced. He looked at the motionless figure of Curly Brennan.

'Have you killed Curly?' he demanded.

'He ain't dead,' Arlen responded. 'The damn fool tried to use his shotgun. I called to him to drop it but he's like you. When he gets it into his head to fight then hell would freeze over before he'd give up.'

Fenner's gaze switched to the motionless Ed Parr, standing in a corner with his hands manacled. The cowboy seemed unhurt.

'What's Parr done?' Fenner asked.

'He resisted arrest when I got here. He was carrying a rifle and seemed inclined to use it although he knows me by sight and I told him I was carrying out my law duties.'

'But you're not acting for the law.' Fenner's head was clearing slowly, his thoughts beginning to flow normally. 'Hegg told me you were in on the steal – you and Tipple together. That's why Jagger killed Hegg. He knew the lawyer would open his mouth to save himself, and that was exactly what Hegg was doing when Jagger opened fire on us without warning.'

Arlen's face changed expression, became ugly with guilt. His smile faded and he levelled his gun at Fenner's head, his finger trembling on the trigger. 'So you're a clever man, huh?' he said. 'You reckon you got all the answers. You think you know how many fleas there are on a dog's hind leg. Well I got one answer you don't know. What you said has put nails in the coffins of Ruthie and

Parr. They heard what you said so I got to kill them along with you. Its no use looking at Chuck and Davis,' he added when Fenner's gaze switched to the two silent possemen. 'They have been working in with me from the moment the steal began.'

'Who else is in it with you?' Fenner asked.

'You know all the answers so you tell me.' Arlen grinned.

'Tipple is the man I planned to see after I'd got to you,' Fenner said. 'I know he started this crooked business.'

'You ain't gonna get to him, and you didn't get to me. I got to you. After all the helling around you've done, you walked in here and practically gave yourself up. As for Tipple, he'll be arriving here any time now. We knew you'd have to come back here sometime, and were prepared to wait. Tipple has got some mighty important business with you.'

Fenner said nothing. His head was aching and he was having trouble keeping his eyes open, but there was nothing wrong with his ears. He had already picked up the sound of hoofs outside in the yard, and although Arlen must have heard them he did not betray the slightest interest. Moments later booted feet sounded on the porch and then the door to the house creaked open.

'Where are you, Arlen?' a voice demanded.

'In here,' the deputy replied.

Fenner looked towards the door and watched Kane Tipple enter the room. The saloonman was wearing a smart store suit. His feet were encased in riding boots, and a low-crowned plains hat was sitting squarely on his head. The fancy gunbelt around his waist held an ornate, pearl-handled pistol holstered on his right hip. He paused in the doorway and looked around, his dark eyes glinting when he saw Fenner sitting on the floor.

'So you got him,' he observed. 'At last you got him.'

'It wasn't too difficult.' Arlen was grinning. 'All that fancy stuff Jagger pulled, and he got nothing right. He got it wrong in the end, too. Fenner killed him. I told you at the start that Jagger was not the man for the job. He let the Quigleys run wild, and couldn't even keep Hegg in his place. You set great store by Jagger but he was only a fast gun with no brain. Fenner ran rings round him, and the rest of them. He shot their lights out. You're gonna have to bring in a whole new outfit to carry on.'

'I disagree. You've got Fenner and that means we've won.' Tipple walked to where Fenner was sitting and gazed down at him, a twisted grin on his thin lips. 'You ran us ragged but you did me a favour by killing Jagger and the Quigleys. It's worked out well, all things considered.'

'There's no one else on the spread,' Arlen cut in. 'Just Fenner and these two to be taken care of. Ruthie certainly came out of her shell after Fenner hit town. She came here to warn him, and finished up at Q Bar. Jagger would have killed her if Fenner hadn't showed up there.'

Fenner was trying to get his brain to work. His thoughts seemed to be stuck in a circular groove, going round and round and making no sense. He put a hand to his left temple. His hat was missing and his fingers touched congealed blood above his ear. A pulse was throbbing painfully in his head. He felt that all he wanted to do was lie down and sleep.

'Shall I take them outside and finish them?' Arlen asked.

'Are you crazy?' Tipple turned on the deputy like a

mountain lion. 'I told you yesterday I wanted Fenner alive. If you kill him he won't be able to sign over the ranch, which means I would have to pay for it. Hegg had the necessary papers prepared weeks ago, and it's a good thing I insisted on keeping them in my possession. There'll be time to kill him after he's signed the bill of sale. We can explain the absence of the money for the sale by saying Hegg got away with it.'

'Except that Hegg didn't get away. Fenner killed him.'

'So we don't know what happened to the money after Hegg collected it.' Tipple spoke irritably. 'Let's get on with it. The papers are in a case on my horse. Have it brought in and we'll settle this business. I don't want anything to go wrong now. Nothing seems to have gone right from the moment Fenner arrived in the county. Get him on his feet and sit him at that table. He looks done for right now, but he should be able to sign his name. Then you can take him out and kill him.'

'Sure.' Arlen grasped Fenner's left arm and began to haul him to his feet, looking towards the crooked deputies as he did so. 'Davis,' he rapped, 'go get Tipple's case.'

Fenner made no effort to get up, pretending that he was unable to do so. His head lolled on his shoulders. His eyes were half closed but he was watching Arlen closely. Arlen was holding his pistol in his right hand, but holstered it as Fenner let his whole weight sag forward. He grasped Fenner with both hands and half dragged, half carried him towards the table. Fenner twisted slightly, pretending to overbalance. Arlen cursed and turned to thrust his right shoulder into Fenner's left armpit to support him.

'For God's sake, Fenner,' he rasped, 'you ain't hurt that bad, are you?'

Fenner reached out his right hand and snatched Arlen's pistol from its holster, at the same time thrusting the deputy away and stepping to his right as his thumb cocked the .45. Arlen cursed in shock and spun, reaching for Fenner's pistol, which he had thrust into his waistband. Fenner kept moving, swinging the gun up and across to level it at Arlen's chest. He saw the deputy in the background lifting his gun, but Arlen was blocking the man's view and he could not fire.

Fenner triggered the gun, blasting a bullet in Arlen's chest as the deputy tried desperately to get into the fight. Still moving to his right, Fenner shifted his aim to the other deputy. His ears were ringing from the crash of the shot. Out of the corner of his eye he saw Tipple running from the room. He fired at the deputy, shaking the room with gun thunder. His pretence was gone now, but he swayed as a bout of dizziness struck him and his sight dimmed.

Tipple had left the room hard on the heels of Davis, who swung round to came back into the room when the shooting erupted. They collided as the saloon man fled. Fenner lurched forward and leaned against the door jamb to steady himself. Tipple had fallen to the floor from his impact with Davis, who was lifting his gun to fight. He and Fenner fired simultaneously. Fenner felt the flashing pain of a slug boring into his left hip. Davis went over backwards, hit in the throat by Fenner's bullet.

Fenner pushed himself upright, covering Tipple, who was clutching the butt of his half-drawn gun, frozen in fear because the muzzle of Fenner's deadly pistol was covering him.

'Go ahead,' Fenner invited. 'Try your luck.'

Tipple paused for an interminable moment, desire showing in his eyes, then he lifted his hand from his gun and raised both hands in token of surrender.

'On your feet.' Fenner felt as if he were about to lose his senses. There was a buzzing in his ears. 'Back in here and free Ed Parr. Arlen will have a handcuffs key in his pocket.'

Tipple got up and hurried into the room. Fenner followed closely, forcing himself to remain on his feet. The room seemed to be spinning and tilting. His sight was receding despite his efforts to remain alert. Tipple seemed to be taking a lifetime getting the key from Arlen, and then Ruth screamed vibrantly, the sound jolting Fenner back to full alertness. He saw Tipple turning around from Arlen's body with a small, two-shot hideout gun in his hand.

Fenner triggered his gun instinctively. The bullet took Tipple in the forehead. Gunsmoke swirled across the room as the saloonman tumbled untidily to the floor. Ed Parr moved into Fenner's circle of vision, holding out his hand for Fenner's gun. Fenner gave it to him, but it wasn't needed. The shooting was over.

Fenner lost everything then. His sense of balance failed and he collapsed without a sound. . . .

It was full daylight when he opened his eyes again, and he was thankful the awful buzzing had left him. His sight was clear and he lifted his head to look around, the movement causing him to groan. He was lying comfortably in a bed. His head ached and there was a throbbing pain in his left hip. A movement beside the bed alerted him and he tensed. Then Ruth stepped into his view, her face showing worry.

'How are you feeling?' she enquired.

'I have felt better,' he admitted. He was aware of a great hunger inside. He felt weak. 'What's happening? How long have I been in bed?'

'Two days.' She smiled. 'The doctor has seen you. He reckons you'll be up on your feet in no time, if you rest properly until you're better. He asked me to stay and make sure you obey his orders. Curly Brennan is making progress. The doctor took him into town in the buckboard. Sheriff Tooke was over from Oak Ridge yesterday. He'll be back to see you when you're able to talk. He said to tell you he's satisfied the trouble is over. Now what can I get you to eat? You've got to build up your strength if you're going to get up and run this ranch.'

'How long will you be staying here?' he asked.

'For as long as you need me,' she replied.

Fenner relaxed, strangely comforted by the knowledge that she would be around. He closed his eyes, needing more sleep. As Ruth had said, he needed to be up on his feet to get on with the work that awaited. He wanted to get the spread into shape before Albie and Bill Blick showed up from Twin Forks, but he felt reluctant to move immediately. He fell into a healing sleep, and Ruth saw a smile soften his craggy face. . . .